I0846691

PATTI JO MOORE

THE KING'S RANSOM

Patti Jo Moore

Published by Forget Me Not Romances, a division of Winged Publications

ISBN-13: 978-1-962168-38-0

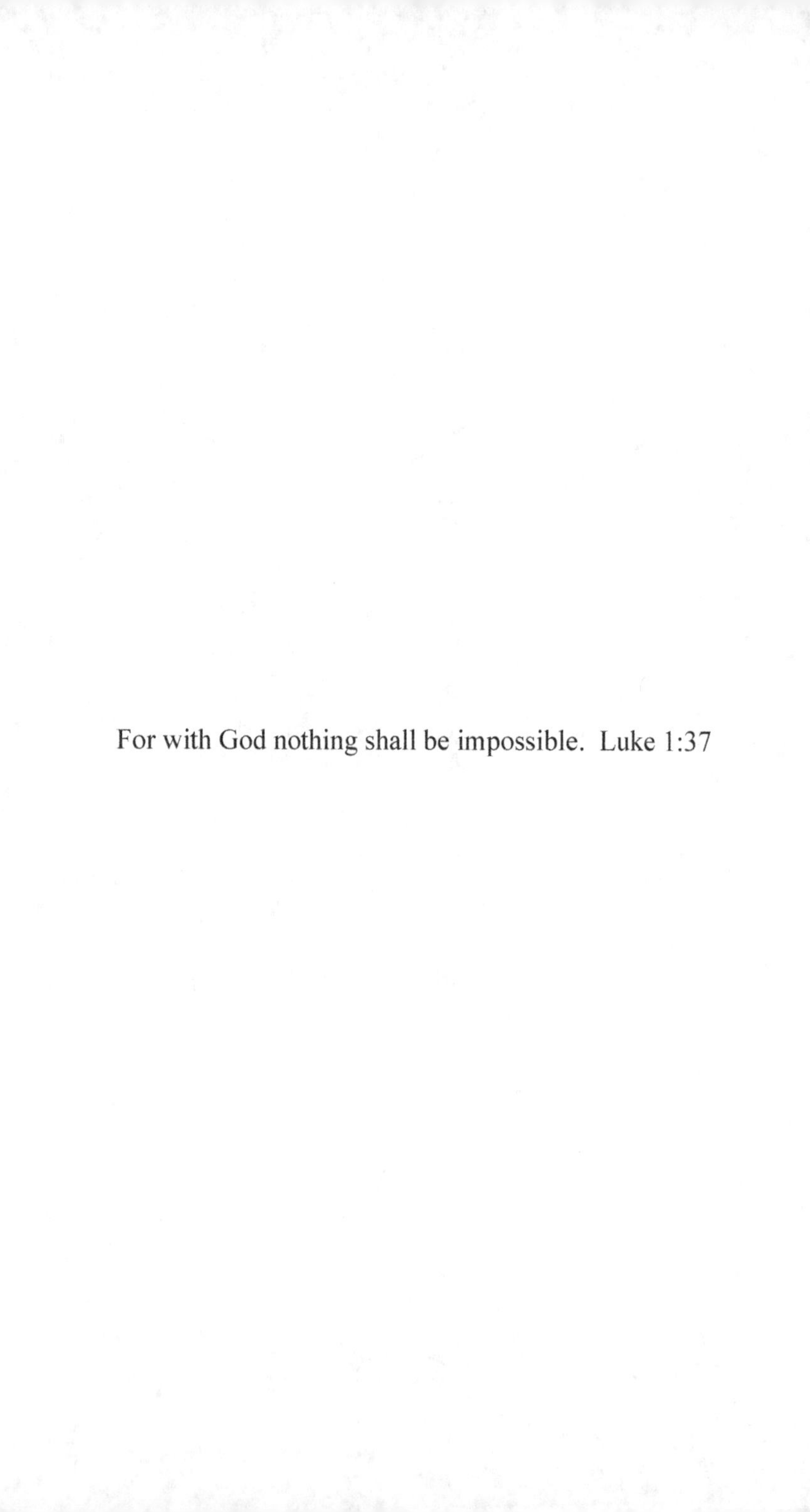

For with God nothing shall be impossible. Luke 1:37

THE KING'S RANSOM

Dedication: This book is lovingly dedicated to my daughter Rebecca, who has always encouraged and supported my love of writing. Mom loves you, Becca!

And to Jesus Christ, my Savior and King, who blesses me beyond measure.

Chapter One

Tina Ransom gripped the armrests of her airplane seat, silently praying the jolts were turbulence and nothing serious. But each time the plane jostled her, Tina's fingernails dug into the vinyl even tighter, as though the seat would save her life.

Deep breaths. Keep praying. But those deep breaths didn't calm her racing heart nor did they prevent her mind from conjuring up images of her late parents, who'd perished in a small plane crash three years ago. Was she destined for the same fate?

"What do you think is happening?" The elderly man seated to Tina's left leaned toward her, his voice raspy. His knuckles were white against the gray.

Tina's heart tugged at the man's taut jawline. Her thoughts switched from worrying about herself to how she might comfort this senior citizen, despite the continued bumpiness of the flight.

Reaching over with her left hand, she gently patted his arm. "We must've hit a rough patch of clouds, but hopefully we'll fly out of this soon." His brow furrowed, so Tina changed the topic. "Is this your first time visiting Italy?" She willed herself to project a calmness she wasn't feeling.

A shaky nod was his reply. Perhaps he'd prefer to sit quietly. Another bump shook them, reminding Tina it was a blessing she'd taken a nausea tablet before boarding the flight. Otherwise, she'd be seaweed green at the moment.

Flying wasn't on her list of favorite things to do, especially after the loss of her parents. But this long-awaited trip to Italy was a dream-come-true, and flying was necessary to achieve her dream. If only her best friend Lucy was with her, then maybe Tina wouldn't be quite so nervous.

How ironic it was that Lucy had planned this trip and encouraged Tina to go, yet now she was stuck back home in Tennessee, ill and unable to travel. Tina suddenly felt all alone. *Get a grip. You're twenty-seven years old, not a little kid.*

Just then the jet lurched forward followed by a plethora of gasps. The pilot had already instructed the passengers to remain seated with their seatbelts fastened since they were experiencing some mild turbulence. If this was mild, she'd hate to think what the armrests would look like for severe turbulence.

Another jolt sent her head against the back of her upright seat. Tina silently recited the twenty-third Psalm, her fingernails still doing their best to keep her alive.

What seemed like an hour, but was actually a few minutes, passed when the ride smoothed. Were they out of the turbulence? Tina closed her eyes and tried to imagine what Italy would be like. She could hardly wait. Her mouth practically watered just thinking about authentic Italian cuisine, and finally experiencing the sights and sounds of a country she'd yearned to visit since she was a child.

The pilot spoke again. "Ladies and gentlemen, we've been cleared to make an emergency landing, so please remain seated and we'll update you as soon as we've safely landed."

Tina was numb. Emergency landing? Her heart pounded. Wasn't this only supposed to happen in movies? She was a kindergarten teacher going on her dream vacation, not an actress. She'd saved for years to be able to afford this trip. Not to mention trying to conquer her fear of flying, which had been a major challenge. This *could not* be happening to her.

Her ears popped. The plane was losing altitude, but at least the passengers weren't being jerked as they'd been earlier. A glance out the window showed the blue ocean below. A *deep* blue ocean.

The plane's speaker crackled. "Ladies and gentlemen, thank you for your cooperation in remaining seated with seatbelts fastened. We will be landing shortly on the island of Felinia and have been granted permission to use their small landing field. I will do my best to make this a smooth landing, and we'll update you as soon as the plane is on the ground. Please continue to remain seated and calm. Thank you."

The speaker went off and the buzz of voices in the plane resumed, becoming louder by the second. *Calm* was not the word to describe the frantic passengers.

The man beside Tina turned to her, his brow again furrowed. "Did the pilot say we're landing in Felinia?"

She nodded, trying again to reassure the elderly gentleman. She had no idea about his health and hoped he wouldn't suffer a heart attack during the shaky flight. "Yes, sir. The pilot sounded certain that we'll be able to land okay." She forced a smile and was relieved when the man smiled in return.

It was obvious the plane was losing altitude rapidly. The voices around Tina became subdued. Eerily quiet. It was as though everyone held their breath, fearful about the emergency landing. Lower and lower…and then BUMP! The jet's tires hit the runway with a squeal as the plane sped along, finally coming to a rough stop.

The passengers cheered, clapped, and a few shrieked. Tina lifted her eyes and uttered, "Thank you, Lord." Then she turned to the older man and patted his arm gently. "We made it, sir. We're on the ground now." To her relief, the color had returned to his face.

He smiled at her with moisture pooling in his eyes. "Yes, we did. Thank you for your kindness, young lady." He reached into his shirt pocket and pulled out a linen handkerchief, then dabbed at his nose and eyes.

The flight attendants were in the aisle, instructing everyone to remain seated. Tina craned her neck to look out the window, hoping to get an idea of their current landscape. A mixture of relief, fear, and disappointment battled inside her. How long would they be on this island that she knew nothing about? She regretted not studying geography more in school.

Although she had a wealth of knowledge about Italy, Tina knew nothing at all about this tiny island perched in the ocean somewhere to the west of Italy.

Her head throbbed and for about the hundredth time since her journey began, she wished Lucy was with her. She would've helped to make this ordeal less frightening, not to mention making her laugh. By now the two of them would've been giggling about this entire fiasco.

One of the flight attendants stopped beside her row and smiled at the older man and then at Tina. "Thank you for your cooperation. You may unfasten your seat belt, and as soon as possible we'll begin exiting the plane. The pilot will be giving instructions."

"Ma'am, how long are we going to be here?" Tina asked before the flight attendant moved on.

Just then, the speaker came on again, and the pilot spoke, weariness evident in his voice. "No worries, ladies and gentlemen. We've landed safely here in Felinia and in a matter of minutes will be exiting the plane. If you have items stored in the overhead compartments, please retrieve those and ask for assistance if needed. You will be directed where to head once you are off the plane."

It seemed all the passengers started talking at once, voicing the same question Tina had.

After a brief pause, the pilot continued, "If this plane is unable to continue the flight, rest assured that our company will send in another craft to continue our last leg of the journey. You and your baggage will be transported safely to Italy, so despite this inconvenience, you will reach your destination. Thank you again for your cooperation in this unexpected delay of our flight."

As the speaker clicked off, the buzz of voices resumed, many of them louder this time. Frustration and worry were obvious in the snippets of conversation Tina overheard. She felt the very same way, but what good was voicing her feelings? Besides, she had no one to express her concerns to except the man seated beside her, and she certainly wasn't going to add to his distress by complaining.

Forcing a perkiness in her voice, Tina smiled and sat up straighter in her seat. "Well, sounds like we'll be getting off here soon, and things will be fine." To her relief, he nodded and returned a smile.

Fifteen minutes later, Tina followed the line of tired passengers into a building. Since they'd gone directly from the plane into an attached tunnel at the country's airport, there wasn't a chance to look around outside. She was eager for a glimpse of this bonus locale that had appeared unexpectedly in her itinerary.

The group was ushered into a lobby area of the small airport—such a contrast from the large, hectic airport in Atlanta! Since she'd overheard a flight attendant telling another passenger that English was spoken in this country, Tina wasn't surprised to see that all the signs in the airport were written in English, in addition to Italian.

One of the flight attendants gestured to a group of chairs. A middle-aged woman she'd noticed on the plane earlier now stood beside her and shook her head. "I don't think this tiny airport has enough seats to accommodate all of us." She scowled before glancing at her watch.

A few moments later the woman turned to Tina. "I sure hope they get our jet repaired soon. I'm eager to see my sister. She's lived in Italy for the past five years and this is my first time flying to visit her. So of course, the plane has trouble." She shook her head.

Tina smiled at her. "I'm sure you'll be glad to see your sister. How long will you be staying in Italy?"

Upon hearing Tina's question, the woman's countenance softened. "Two weeks, and I've really been looking forward to this trip. I'm eager to see my sibling, but I also adore Italian food." The woman grinned, her face relaxing. "What about you? Are you going to Italy to visit anyone?"

Tina shook her head, then launched into a brief explanation of her pleasure trip. "It's been a dream of mine since I was a young child. My late parents visited Italy before I was born, and they shared pictures with me. My best friend Lucy was supposed to accompany me, but at the last minute she became very ill."

Now the woman reached out and patted her arm. "I'm sorry your friend had to miss the trip, but you can share your adventures with her when you return home. By the way, my name is Jeanette. Jeanette Forrester."

"Nice to meet you, Jeanette. I'm Tina Ransom, from Blueberry Cove, Tennessee."

"Ah, I knew I detected a southern accent. I guess you can tell I'm from New York."

For the next fifteen minutes, Tina and her new friend visited, each one sharing a little about their hometowns. Turned out, Jeanette had taught school years ago, so she appeared delighted when Tina mentioned being a kindergarten teacher.

Just then one of the flight attendants stepped up to them and smiled, belying her tired eyes. "The airline has another plane enroute here to finish our flight to Italy, so we will need to remain here in Felinia a while longer. We will notify you when the replacement aircraft arrives." With a polite nod, the flight attendant then moved on to another cluster of passengers to relay the update.

Jeanette's brow furrowed. "Wonder why they don't just make the announcement with a loudspeaker? Then everyone could hear at once."

"I'm not sure, but my guess is that they figure the news will be more comforting if the flight attendants speak directly with a few passengers at a time."

Jeanette nodded. "That sounds right." The woman sat back in her chair, obviously more at ease now. "Since we have time, how about telling me about your life in Tennessee? I'm sure you lead a more exciting life than I do." She chuckled.

Tina giggled. "I'm not sure I'd call my life exciting, but I do love teaching kindergarten. In the summers I do volunteer work at my church and that keeps me busy too. My parents have both passed away." She paused, fighting a lump trying to form in her throat.

Jeanette again patted her arm. "I'm so sorry, dear. And you're so young. Did they pass away recently?" Compassion was evident in her tone.

"It was three years ago. They were in a small plane that crashed while visiting friends in Texas. It was very hard, but I know I'll see them in Heaven one day." She fought back the tears that threatened to form, then she continued, "I have one brother who also lives in Tennessee, and he's happy I'm taking this trip. I don't want to alarm him by letting him know about the emergency landing, so I'll wait and phone him when we've landed in Italy."

"That sounds wise. I'll notify my sister of our

delay after awhile. You've helped me calm down, Tina, and I appreciate that. I'm not sure if you could tell, but when we first got off the plane I was not a happy camper." Jeanette shrugged.

Tina smiled. At least the woman was truthful.

Twenty minutes later the group of passengers received another update about their flight. The replacement jet should be arriving within four hours, so they had time to walk around the small airport if they chose.

Soon the crew began handing out chips, cookies, and canned drinks to the passengers. Tina couldn't help feeling sorry for the flight crew. After all, the plane's malfunction wasn't their fault, and they had to be exhausted by this point in the journey.

Jeanette opened her small bag of chips. "Did you see the large paintings of the king and prince when we first entered the airport?"

"Yes, I did. It's odd but I've never even heard about this island. I wonder if the king knows about our emergency landing?"

"Hmm…I'd think they would've been notified about us. But I was thinking how handsome the prince is. I'm trying to remember what I've read about him in the news. Nothing scandalous, but there was a small article I saw a while back. Little did I know then that I'd be visiting his country." Jeanette laughed before taking a sip of her canned cola.

After eating, Tina, Jeanette, and some of the other passengers strolled around the small airport, admiring the posters on the walls that featured paintings of the castle. Although her older friend seemed eager to return to their seats, Tina wanted to continue walking around a bit. It felt good to stretch her legs after sitting so long.

After Jeanette left to return to her seat, Tina ambled along a wide corridor, admiring the paintings interspersed with actual photographs. Surprisingly, she found herself yearning to see this island, rather than only the airport. *Well, maybe someday I can plan a visit here and be a tourist. With the small size it probably wouldn't take long to see the entire island.*

Tina glanced at her watch, not knowing the actual time. She'd better return to the lobby and sit with Jeanette. The older woman might be concerned if Tina stayed too long in the corridor area. Besides, it was most likely almost time for the replacement jet to arrive.

A renewed excitement bubbled up inside her as she again thought of reaching Italy. Finally! Her dream trip was coming true. Yet, a little part of her longed to remain there in Felinia.

~ ~ ~

"Tell me again what happened, Wentworth." King Franklin huffed out a sigh and shook his head. "Some jibberish about a jet landing here on our island due to an emergency?"

Prince Reginald sat off to the side, observing the interaction between his father and Wentworth, their personal assistant, whose well-intentioned ways often irritated his father.

"Certainly, Your Majesty." The late forties man cleared his throat and spoke more slowly this time, explaining that he'd been notified of a jet from the United States requesting to land on Felinia due to an emergency.

The king nodded and stroked his whiskered chin. "I see. Well, I certainly hope everyone aboard the jet is safe and the landing went smoothly. But what I don't follow are your earlier comments about security concerns. Please clarify that, Wentworth."

The assistant's face turned crimson, and he cleared his throat yet again, now appearing a bit uncomfortable. "Um, yes, Sire. Those comments were merely my own observations and concerns about the safety of our country. We need to make certain that our unexpected visitors are all trustworthy." He ducked his head briefly, still obviously embarrassed as the king stared at him.

Prince Reginald spoke up, mainly to forestall his father's agitation, but also because he felt a wee bit of pity for poor Wentworth. The man meant well but often over-reacted, which only added to King Franklin's irritability.

"Wentworth, I'm sure my father would agree with me that we appreciate your concern for our country's protection, but surely the passengers on the jet are not a threat. After all, it was an emergency landing, not something that was planned." He didn't want to further embarrass Wentworth, but the man didn't need to jump to conclusions that were way off.

"Yes, Sire. I'm sure you are correct. I was simply looking out for the citizens of Felinia." He stiffened and lifted his chin.

King Franklin spoke again, his earlier irritability somewhat soothed. "Thank you, Wentworth. We all appreciate your diligence in keeping an eye on situations, but as my son has said, the passengers who were forced to land on our island are surely not any kind of threat. However, we need to make certain they are treated well while they're here." He nodded, a signal of dismissal.

Wentworth took the cue and bowed, then turned and exited the room.

Reginald couldn't suppress a grin. "Poor Wentworth. I know he means well, but so often he assumes the negative in situations." He shook his head.

"Yes, that he does. But he is such a loyal staff member, which is why he's remained in our service all these years." The king hesitated, then peered at his son. "You don't suppose his concerns hold any merit, do you? From the way much of our world is behaving these days, I know there are many evil people out there who do wish to harm those in other countries." The king stroked his graying whiskers.

"Father, are you being taken in by Wentworth's paranoid nature?" Reginald offered a playful tsk-tsk, hoping to lighten the mood. As the king was aging, it seemed that he took matters to heart more than he had when younger, and Reginald certainly didn't want him to be troubled.

King Franklin waved a dismissive hand. "No, but I do think we need to keep abreast of the world around us. We certainly don't want any repeats of war or conflicts as we've had in the past." A frown furrowed his brow.

Reginald stepped close and patted his shoulder. "Father, I seriously doubt we need to worry, no matter how many countries might be at war. No reason to think we'll repeat the late 1800s." He was certain the war that affected the tiny island in the last years of the nineteenth century were on his father's mind. He forced an upbeat tone. "Besides, the countries that Felinia battled then are now allies, in the strongest sense."

His words obviously relieved the king, because he visibly relaxed and reached for the bell to ring for tea. "You're right, my son. Will you join me in a cup of tea? I've been fighting a pesky headache all day and it's not easing. Perhaps more tea will help."

Reginald moved closer to his father and frowned. "Have you taken a dose of your headache medicine?"

The king nodded. "A small dose, so if this tea doesn't help, I may need another dose. Perhaps even an afternoon nap." He chuckled, then looked at his son with a hint of nostalgia in his dark eyes. "Ah, Reginald. When I was your age, I never needed a nap or even a rest time during the day. But now I grow weary more quickly. Signs of getting old, for certain."

A tug at Reginald's heart made him want to reassure his father. "Father, you are not old. You've worked hard leading a country for many years, and it's only natural for you to feel weary at times. You are wise to rest when you feel the need. After all, the Bible tells us that even Jesus got away and rested." He grinned at his father. Reginald was fiercely loyal to the man seated a few feet away.

King Franklin smiled as the petite maid knocked before entering the room with the tea. After she bowed first at the king and then the prince, she inquired if Reginald would also like a cup of tea.

"No thank you, Hilda. I appreciate your offer though. My father has a headache, so he might need his medicine or a cold compress for his head later on." Reginald grinned, expecting his father to protest. Instead, the king sent an appreciative smile to his son, then carefully took the cup of hot tea from the maid.

Hilda bowed again, assuring Reginald she'd be checking on the king again soon. Then she left the room. Reginald always chuckled at her mouse-like behavior, and had tried to help her feel more at ease. But she was from an old family of servants, so she continued the tradition of showing the utmost respect for authority.

Turning to exit his father's keeping room, Reginald was struck with an idea. He faced his father again. "Father, do you think it might be a good idea if I greeted the visitors who made the emergency landing on our island? Perhaps just a few words of welcome and telling them to have a safe trip to Italy."

King Franklin set his teacup down and he nodded. "I think that's an excellent suggestion, my son. If you don't mind doing so, just a few words of welcome and please give them my regards. I hate to mention this, but perhaps it might be a good idea to say that I'd speak to them myself but I'm not feeling my best today."

Reginald nodded. "Thank you. I will certainly do so, and you need to rest and not worry about a thing." He didn't mention Wentworth's earlier concerns about the visitors. No need to stir up fears that held no basis.

Stepping into the hallway, Reginald saw Wentworth standing nearby, ever the sentry. The very thought almost brought a smile, but that would make the assistant wonder what was going on. So he maintained a serious demeanor and spoke.

"I've discussed this matter with the king, and he's in full agreement, Wentworth. I'm going to address our visitors before they continue on their journey to Italy. It will be a fitting gesture, don't you think?"

Wentworth appeared pleased that his opinion had been asked, and his face lit up. "Oh yes, sire. A very nice gesture indeed. Excellent idea." The two men walked slowly along the hallway, discussing arrangements for the royal car to take them from the castle to the airport, which was only a distance of six miles.

Reginald hurried to his quarters on the second floor, eager to have this task taken care of. Not that he was nervous, but he would be representing the country of Felinia, so he needed to prepare what he'd say.

In his quarters, he quickly dressed in one of his suitable uniforms and sat down at a table to write a brief speech. But first he prayed. His mother—God rest her soul—had instilled in him a deep faith in God. She'd also taught him the importance of seeking the Lord's help in even the smallest tasks.

By the time he met Wentworth to ride to the airport, Reginald felt calm and almost excited at the opportunity to act as an ambassador to a group of strangers from America.

~ ~ ~

Chapter 2

Tina stood to stretch her legs just as Jeanette came bustling back from the ladies' room. "Did you hear the news?" The middle-aged woman was breathless and her eyes large with excitement.

"Is our replacement jet here?" Tina was more than ready to continue the flight to Italy to start her dream trip.

Jeanette shook her head. "No, I haven't heard any new updates about the jet. But I did hear that someone from Felinia's royal family is going to be speaking to us very soon. Isn't that exciting? Maybe the king." She paused a moment as if searching her memory for a name. Then she brightened. "Oh yes, King Franklin. Maybe it will be the king himself who speaks to us. How thrilling." She clasped her hands together and beamed.

"No, I haven't heard anything about that. Wow, a real king speaking to us. That is exciting!" Now she wished that she'd taken more of an interest in European geography in the sixth grade. Why didn't she know anything about this tiny island nation? After all, it wasn't that far off the coast of the country of her dreams.

Word spread quickly, and soon the group of passengers was buzzing with talk of a royal family member speaking to them. Tina secretly hoped that if the king spoke to them, maybe he'd have his son standing with him. The painting of Prince Reginald had shown a very handsome man, and seeing him in person would be a nice bonus to her trip.

Within minutes, the flight attendants asked everyone to take a seat and to remain quiet as someone from Felinia's royal family welcomed them. Many of the passengers—Tina included—held cameras ready to snap a photo of royalty.

The air was thick with excitement, and a few minutes later a loud voice proclaimed the entry of Prince Reginald of Felinia. *The Prince!* It was all Tina could do to stay seated, as she yearned to stand up and crane her neck for a closer look. Even from a distance she saw the resemblance of the live man to the handsome man in the painting.

Appearing a bit shy, Prince Reginald stepped up to a microphone that had been set up for him on a small podium. He was surrounded by several men, presumably guards to keep him safe. His uniform was quite striking, bearing a sash with the Felinia coat of arms in the bright colors of green, yellow, and blue. With his tanned skin, dark hair, and deep-set dark eyes, Prince Reginald made an appealing sight.

Was it Tina's imagination, or did Prince Reginald pause when his eyes gazed in her direction? Surely, she was being silly. He was merely taking an overall look at the unexpected visitors in his country and was doing his best to appear pleasant and welcoming. Yet…it did seem that his eyes locked with Tina's for a few seconds, and her heart skipped a beat.

Oh, good grief. You've read too many romance novels. Why on earth would he notice you? The silent scolding in her mind snapped Tina out of any fanciful thoughts, and she realized Jeanette was speaking to her.

"I'm sorry, Jeanette. What did you say?" She leaned closer to hear the woman as the applause died down after the Prince's brief speech. To her dismay Tina saw that he was already being escorted out of the lobby area by the guardsmen who'd stood around him as he spoke.

"I was just saying the prince is a fine-looking man, don't you think?" Jeanette's eyes twinkled. Yes, Tina was seeing a different side to this woman who'd earlier seemed quite ornery.

"Yes, he's very handsome." Before she could question the woman, Jeanette offered information she'd gleaned in articles she'd read about the royal family, including the fact that Prince Reginald was supposedly betrothed to a young lady named Lorie.

"From what I've read, the Balfours are a fairly private royal family, and prefer to keep a low profile. Which is a good thing, with all the crazy tabloids out there that love to take the smallest detail and blow it out of proportion."

She shook her head. "Anyway, Prince Reginald and this woman named Lorie are supposedly betrothed, and I can only imagine what a lavish wedding that will be! I have no idea when their wedding is supposed to take place, but I hope some of the photos will be shared with the public."

For a reason she didn't understand, Tina felt a twinge of disappointment at hearing the prince was engaged. It made no sense for her to feel that way. She pasted a smile on her face. "Wow, I'm sure that will be a gorgeous wedding. Is Lorie from a royal family? I'm not sure how all that works, but I thought royalty was supposed to marry royalty."

"You know, I'm not sure either. I'm trying to recall what I've read about the woman he's betrothed to, and all I can remember reading is her name and she's close to the prince's age." Jeanette frowned. "I'll have to see what information I can dig up on her."

At that moment, the flight attendants came around again to inform the passengers that the replacement jet should arrive within the hour. "You still have time to visit the restrooms or walk around if you choose. But please try to return to this area in no more than forty-five minutes." The flight attendant smiled, though her eyes reflected fatigue, then she moved on to repeat her announcement.

Tina stood and stretched. "I think I will walk around again for a little bit. Would you like to join me?"

Jeanette grinned and shook her head, then pulled a paperback from her tote bag. "No, I'll just sit and read, because once we board the plane for Italy, I'll be too excited to read, I'm sure."

Tina smiled and headed toward the wall of glass windows that overlooked the small runway. Other passengers huddled here and there, their voices speculating about how long it would take to reach Italy from Felinia. Everyone else appeared as tired as she was. Hopefully, there would be time on the continuing flight for a cat nap.

She headed down the hallway where the restrooms and snack machines were located, waving at fellow passengers she passed. What were their reasons for traveling to Italy? She supposed most were going for a vacation, although a couple of the male passengers appeared to be businessmen who were likely traveling for their jobs.

Lost in thought, Tina hadn't been paying attention to how far she'd walked, but now noticed she'd gone beyond the restroom and snack area. There were several closed doors that she assumed must be offices.

Suddenly one of the doors opened. Tina jumped, feeling like a child who'd wandered into an off-limits area of a museum. Two men exited the room. One of the men was Prince Reginald!

She gasped and her face warmed. *Why hadn't she been paying attention to where she was walking?* Resisting the urge to turn around and run, she slowed down. It would certainly be even more embarrassing if she tripped and fell.

"Hello. Are you looking for someone?" The prince spoke directly to her.

Tina wasn't sure if she should curtsy or bow, so she slightly bent forward.

The prince gazed at her with amusement evident in his dark eyes. His *very handsome* dark eyes. The middle-aged man standing beside him clearly was *not* amused, if the scowl on his face was any indication.

Tina moistened her lips and mustered a smile. "N-No sir, I was taking a walk to stretch my legs. But I'm afraid I've walked too far, and I apologize. I-I'm Tina

Ransom from Tennessee." For a split-second, she wondered if she needed to show some identification. After all, she was a stranger in the presence of royalty.

The prince raised a hand as though to reassure her. "No need to apologize. We want you to feel welcome in Felinia. Isn't that correct, Wentworth?" He slid his gaze to the man beside him before returning his attention to Tina.

The man named Wentworth cleared his throat and nodded, although still slightly scowling. "Certainly, Your Highness." He clasped his hands behind his back, and for a moment, Tina wondered if he did so in an effort to keep from throttling her.

"I'll return to my group in the lobby." Tina swung around to return the way she'd come, but the prince's words stopped her cold.

"Oh, there's no need to rush off. Do you have some time before your flight leaves for Italy?" As soon as the prince asked the question, Wentworth's eyebrows shot up.

But the prince didn't give his assistant time to offer input. "If you do, then perhaps you'd like to learn a little more about our small, but fascinating, country." His smile sent Tina's insides into melting mode. What if she collapsed right here on the floor? She needed to think clearly, but this was all so surreal.

"I do have about thirty minutes, Your Highness." Given the prince's handsome looks, she'd be content to sit and stare at him for her remaining time in Felinia.

The prince gestured with his right hand, indicating they'd continue on down the hallway. "We can head to a room here in the airport that houses some information about Felinia. Perhaps one day you'll want to return to our small country rather than just make an emergency landing here." His eyes softened as he looked at her. "I'm sure that must have been frightening for you and the other passengers." He slowed his steps while awaiting her reply.

She nodded. "Yes, Sire. It certainly was."

He chuckled and leaned toward her ever so slightly. "I appreciate your politeness, Miss Ransom, but you really don't need to say 'sire' to me. As I feel quite certain we're close to the same age." He winked and cast a swift glance at Wentworth, who was still clearly *not* amused.

Tina was suddenly aware of the prince's height. He appeared to be well over six feet. Handsome *and* tall.

"If you'd like, we'll step into the room that displays some of our memorabilia. I know you have a time limit, but I hope you'll enjoy perusing some of our displays." A note of pride was evident in his tone.

A minute later, Tina stood in awe as she gazed around the large room. Countless pictures—both photographs and paintings—hung along each wall. Prince Reginald proudly gave a condensed overview of his country's history, pointing out various ancestors in several of the paintings. There was even a timeline of sorts on one wall, displaying the history of Felinia from the 1700s to the present day. Tina didn't miss the fact that most of the pictures featured cats in addition to the royal family members.

"This is all so interesting. I really wish I had more time to view everything." Amazement flooded her mind, and her heart yearned to know more about this tiny, but intriguing, island. Tina would savor this moment forever and could hardly wait to tell Lucy. *She probably won't even believe me! This is like a magical dream.*

Just as the clock had struck midnight for Cinderella, Tina's mesmerizing moment abruptly ended when Wentworth cleared his throat. "Your Majesty, I do hate to interfere with your visit, but I believe it's time for your guest to return to her fellow passengers. We wouldn't want her to miss her flight."

Tina looked at her cell phone screen and released a small gasp. She didn't have much time at all. A sudden longing to stay right where she was overtook her, but missing her flight was not an option.

"Thank you so much, Prince Reginald. This has been a wonderful and enlightening visit. I've already learned so much about your country, and I'm sure you're proud of Felinia. Thank you for your kindness." Again, not knowing if she should curtsy or bow, she simply nodded toward the prince and smiled.

"This has been my pleasure. I'll admit I'm always eager to show off my country and her history to any guests we have, so I've truly enjoyed this. Now promise me you'll come back and visit Felinia when you can stay longer." A dark eyebrow arched ever so slightly, giving the prince a playful expression.

Tina's heart beat as wildly as hummingbird wings. "I would love that." With a quick wave, she hoisted her handbag over her shoulder and turned to head back to the lobby area, still in a state of disbelief at what had just transpired. *Wait until Jeanette hears about Tina's visit with the prince. She would likely be giddy!*

"There you are. I was getting worried about you."

Jeanette rushed up to her the instant Tina entered the lobby. "Are you okay? I was about to search for you." Jeanette eyed her curiously. "What happened? You look as if you just won a million dollars." The older woman laughed.

"Even better, but I'll have to talk fast because it looks like they're about to begin boarding us on the replacement jet."

In a lowered but excited voice, Tina attempted to sum up her meeting with Prince Reginald, but she could scarcely finish a sentence before her friend would squeal or gasp. In addition to that, Jeanette had reached out to grab Tina's arm in amazement and was now squeezing tightly as Tina spoke.

Tina was afraid Jeanette's grip would cut off her circulation if she didn't release her arm, so she gently loosened Jeanette's hold on her. Her friend cringed and apologized. "This is just so unbelievable. What an adventure. I wish I'd been with you." She shook her head.

"I know. Wish you'd been with me, too, because as exciting as it was, I was very nervous. And the man with the prince kept scowling, so I felt like I was doing something wrong, even though I knew I wasn't." She shrugged.

At that moment the announcement was made that boarding would begin. "Get your ticket ready, because they announced while you were gone that we still have to show proof we're supposed to be on this plane."

With shaky hands, Tina dug into her handbag for her ticket. Before boarding the aircraft, Jeanette handed her a small piece of paper with her contact information on it. "I'd like to keep in touch with you, Tina. You remind me of my dear niece, and you've made this layover stop much more pleasant." Then she bestowed a quick hug around her neck and her eyes brimmed with tears.

To her surprise, Tina felt the same way. Within a few hours, she had grown to feel a true friendship with the woman who was old enough to be her mother. She grinned and squeezed Jeanette's arm. "We'll keep in touch." Then they took their places in line to board the jet.

As the new aircraft lifted off the Felinia airport runway headed to Italy, Tina craned her neck to catch a glimpse of the tiny island country. She knew in her heart she'd visit again. Maybe sooner rather than later.

~ ~ ~

"Sire, with all due respect, do you think that was a good idea earlier today?"

Reginald forced a smile and kept his bristling emotions in check. Some days Wentworth was harder to deal with than other days. The assistant meant well, but often went to the extreme in his fierce protection of the royal family he served.

"I see no harm in making a visitor to Felinia feel welcome, Wentworth. And I hardly think that young lady was a spy attempting to scope out top-secret information. Not that our small country has much of that to contend with, thankfully." Reginald chuckled, hoping Wentworth would loosen up a bit.

"Very well, Sire. I'm only looking out for the safety and well-being of the Balfour family and the country of Felinia."

"I know you are, and I appreciate it greatly."

Reginald reached out and patted the stiff man on the shoulder.

Thankfully, Wentworth left the prince's office to tend to other duties, so Reginald was left alone with his private thoughts. *Tina.* Such a lovely name, and such a lovely lady she was. Reginald blew out a sigh, surprised at his feelings for an American woman he'd only met briefly and knew nothing about. In fact, he most likely would never see her again. That thought caused a tug at his heart.

He plopped down into his chair and, sinking his face into his hands, Reginald silently prayed. *Oh Lord, why did that lady step into my life for only a matter of minutes? I was so drawn to her, though I know nothing about her except her name and her home country.*

Lifting his head, he opened his eyes and gazed out a side window onto the small courtyard that offered a peaceful view. Rosebushes and flowering shrubs lined up on either side, and a large, stone birdbath stood in the center of the yard. So tranquil, unlike his spirit. After all, he was betrothed to Lorie DeVenes. *She* was the woman who should be on his mind. But she wasn't.

In fact, when Reginald did allow his mind to think of Lorie, a sense of dread filled him. He was not looking forward to a marriage with a woman he felt no love for, and that terrified him. But things had happened so quickly with his father taking charge, and before he realized what was happening, King Franklin had assumed that his son was in love with Lorie. Then her father had become close friends with the king, almost forming a partnership of sorts. *What a mess.* How could Reginald have allowed this to go so far?

Tapping at his office door pulled him away from

his miserable thoughts. "Yes, enter please." He attempted to paste a pleasant smile on his face as the maid entered.

"So sorry to bother you, Your Highness, but it's time for afternoon tea." She carefully placed a tray with tea and shortbread cookies on a small table nearby.

"Thank you, Hilda. I appreciate this very much." He smiled warmly at the maid as she bowed and then scurried from the room. Reginald eyed the treats placed before him. The fine china teacup and saucer had delicately-painted red roses on them, and the shortbread cookies were arranged on a plate of the same pattern. A neatly folded linen napkin sat beside the plate of cookies. A nice snack, but it would be even nicer if he had someone to join him.

Unexpectedly, the image of Tina appeared in his mind. Why did he continue thinking of the beautiful woman with the soft drawl? The way she'd gazed up at him with a mixture of shyness and appreciation had made her appear almost vulnerable. The kind of woman he'd want to protect and shield in his arms. Whoa! Guilt coursed through him as he again reminded himself that his thoughts should be on Lorie.

His fiancée was attractive enough and a nice lady. But that was it. He felt no sparks when he was with her. And yet now they were betrothed. What was he going to do? Again, he bowed his head and prayed silently, then forced himself to enjoy the tea and cookies while gazing out his window. Birds splashed in the birdbath and a breeze rustled the branches. The view was soothing and that's what he needed right now. So why was he secretly wishing that Tina was seated beside him also enjoying this view?

If Reginald was completely honest with himself, he knew most likely he'd never see her again. If he only had the chance to get to know her better, perhaps they could be friends. Trouble was, he knew that he'd want to go beyond friendship with her. As he bit into another shortbread cookie and watched a bluebird splashing in the water, he had a feeling his heart was in big trouble.

~ ~ ~

Italy. Tina had finally arrived in the country she'd dreamed of for so many years. The chance to finally see for herself the sights that her parents had told her about almost took her breath away, even as a twinge of sadness pulled at her heart. She still missed them so much but knew without a doubt they would be thrilled she was here.

Surprisingly, she found herself also missing the older woman she'd befriended on their unplanned stop in Felinia, but Jeanette's relatives had most likely whisked her away after landing. She hoped her new friend would have an enjoyable time in Italy. Tina did plan to keep in touch with her.

"Miss? May I help you?" A middle-aged uniformed man eyed her with a bit of concern.

Smiling at the man, Tina asked where the baggage claim area was located. She should've stayed with some of her fellow passengers on the plane, but when they'd disembarked, she'd been so beside herself, she practically wandered around in a daze. No wonder this kind worker asked if she needed help.

He nodded, then told her to follow him. The man led the way to an escalator that bore a large sign overhead, indicating the baggage claim area was downstairs. "Do you need me to take you to the area, or do you think you can locate it?" He asked politely, although Tina figured he likely thought she needed help.

"Thank you, sir. I should be able to find it." She smiled sweetly, then hoisted her handbag higher on her shoulder and stepped carefully onto the escalator. Once she had her baggage and arrived at her hotel, she'd feel a huge amount of relief. Yet she still regretted that Lucy wasn't here with her, and Tina fought the niggle of guilt that her best friend was missing the trip, even though emergency surgery couldn't be helped.

The shuttle ride to her hotel went smoothly and Tina tried to take in all the sights as the small bus drove into the city. She still couldn't believe she was actually in Rome. Amazing! Trying to ignore any nervousness about being alone, Tina forced herself to focus on the passing scenes. Locals riding bikes and street vendors were out in abundance, and it was quite evident she wasn't in her small Tennessee hometown.

Thirty minutes later, she was standing in her hotel room, which offered a nice view of the street below. She could hardly wait to begin exploring, but knew she needed to grab a bite to eat. Not to mention she was tired. *Very* tired.

Maybe in the morning she'd visit the small café located inside her hotel, but for now she'd eat some snacks she'd brought along in her bag. Sitting by the window, Tina munched a granola bar and crackers, then drank the bottled juice she'd purchased in the airport.

No longer hungry, she watched dusk settle over the city. As eager as she was to get out and walk around, Tina decided to stay put and head out sightseeing the next morning. Twenty minutes later she was in the soft bed, still amazed that she'd arrived in Italy. Slumber overtook her, filled with dreams of a handsome prince who begged her to return to his country.

~ ~ ~

Chapter 3

"Buongiorno." **Tina greeted** the hotel workers politely, hoping it wasn't overly obvious that she was a first-time tourist in their country. Everyone seemed cordial and most smiled as they made eye contact with her. The hotel desk clerk proved to be very helpful in suggesting travel sites and services for her to use, and her first two days went surprisingly smoothly as she toured areas of Rome with total strangers. Seeing the Colosseum was even more amazing than she'd thought it would be, and the Pantheon was also a spectacular sight.

Tina kept her text messages to Lucy brief, not wanting to make her friend feel even worse about missing the trip. She focused mainly on asking Lucy how she was feeling and promised that before long they would take a trip together.

The next morning, Tina awakened refreshed and ready to tackle a day of sightseeing, hoping to find a special souvenir to take home to Lucy. As she stopped at the desk to get more suggestions from the friendly hotel clerk, a small poster on the wall behind the counter grabbed her attention. She'd not noticed it previously, but now it held her spellbound. The poster was advertising the small island country of Felinia.

"Buongiorno." The friendly forty-something man smiled warmly at her, as amusement shown in his dark eyes. "Ah, something has captured your attention, yes?" He followed her gaze to the poster on the wall.

Tina chuckled. *"Buongiorno, Luigi.* I don't remember seeing that poster before now."

The hotel clerk laughed and explained he'd only put it up that morning. "It seems our small neighbor out in the sea is wanting to increase their tourism business. Since I have a cousin who lives on Felinia, I told him I would gladly put up a poster." Realization must've dawned on the man because he grinned. "Your plane had to land there on your way here, is that correct?"

She nodded and briefly told him about the emergency landing on the small island. She decided it best to leave out the part about meeting the prince. Her face was sure to turn crimson if she did.

"Yes, one of my co-workers told me about that. But how wonderful that everyone was safe. And you were able to visit another country—even briefly." Luigi turned toward the poster again, then looked back at Tina. "So would you like to visit Felinia again, do you think?"

Tina was beginning to wonder if he could read her mind, or at least tell from the expression on her face that there was something about the country that fascinated her. She swallowed and kept her voice level. "Yes, I would like to visit again. Unfortunately, we only saw a tiny bit of Felinia, since we remained in the airport the entire time. But looking out the window of the plane gave me a view of some lovely land. It appeared lush and green." She'd better be careful and not mention the information she'd gleaned while admiring the displays with the prince.

Luigi brightened and held up a finger. "I have an idea, Miss. When you return from sightseeing, why don't you see me again here at the counter. I will have more information for you if you would like to visit Felinia in the future. But for now, enjoy your day here in beautiful Rome." Another hotel guest had stepped to the counter, so Tina thanked him and turned to head out the door.

After shopping and sightseeing, Tina sat in a small café later that day, enjoying minestrone soup and bread. Luigi's words drifted back to her. It wouldn't hurt to see what information he would share with her, and maybe in the future Lucy could accompany her for a trip to Felinia.

A message came through on her phone, and Tina smiled when she saw it was from Jeanette. Her older friend was checking on her and hoped she was having fun. Tina messaged back a friendly reply, making sure to inquire about Jeanette's visit with her sister. When she left the café, she hurried to a nearby gift shop, eager to purchase a nice souvenir for Lucy.

Returning to her hotel, Tina felt a satisfaction in her day. She'd done a good deal of sightseeing, found a lovely turquoise necklace for Lucy, and enjoyed a delicious meal at a local café. Entering the hotel lobby, she immediately spotted Luigi behind the counter, and he wasn't assisting another guest.

"Buona sera, Luigi." Tina made certain to use the

appropriate greeting, since it was now evening. She set her package on the counter, sudden fatigue weighing her down.

"Buona sera, Miss Ransom." He seemed genuinely pleased to see her, as if encountering an old friend. "And how was your day of sightseeing?"

She briefly described her day, and then gestured to her small package explaining that she'd purchased a gift for her friend. Tina hoped Luigi remembered his comment about offering information on Felinia.

"Sounds like a wonderful day. Now, I have some information for you about Felinia, if you are interested." A twinkle in his eyes caused Tina to wonder if he truly did sense her interest in the country. Or more specifically, the *prince* of that country.

Luigi held out a paper containing handwritten notes. "I am certain your plans are to return to America when you leave Italy in a few days. But if you should decide to stop in Felinia on your return trip to America, here is some information for you." He paused and studied her.

Tina was stunned. This busy hotel clerk had taken the time to gather specific details for her, including the airfare price to Felinia from Rome. Was this a sign that she was supposed to visit the tiny island again? Maybe even on her way home to Tennessee?

~ ~ ~

Prince Reginald drummed his fingers on the book he'd been reading. It was no use. He couldn't focus on his reading or really much of anything lately. For the past few days it seemed that his mind only wanted to return to thoughts of the lady he'd met from America.

Tina. She'd been on her way to Italy, so most likely she was now having a wonderful time. For all he knew she had a fiancé there—or maybe in America. Besides, he shouldn't be thinking of any woman except Lorie.

A tapping sounded at his office door, so he placed the book on his desk and stood. "Please enter." He looked up as Wentworth stepped in and closed the door behind him.

"I'm sorry to disturb you, Sire, but your father asked me to relay a message to you. The banquet that was to be held this Saturday will need to be re-scheduled, as Miss DeVene's father will be away on business." Wentworth paused to await Reginald's response.

"Thank you, Wentworth. I'll make a note on my calendar." He didn't dare reveal how relieved he was at this news.

After Wentworth left his office, Reginald collapsed into his chair and pulled his calendar toward him. Why did he have a feeling of satisfaction as he crossed out the scheduled banquet for the coming Saturday? A stab of guilt prodded him. Yet, the cancellation meant he would not have to be with Lorie and her parents this weekend. He could relax—at least for the time being.

He sank his head into his hands and prayed. *Dear Lord, what am I to do? My father is counting on my marriage to this fine lady, yet the fact remains I do not love her. Yet because I'm to become the king in the not-too-distant future, I need a wife. It's expected of me. Please show me what to do.*

His eyes landed on the small, framed photo of his mother. How he missed her. If she were still alive, he'd be discussing this matter with her. But cancer had cut her life short four years ago, and the entire kingdom had grieved her passing. Reginald could almost hear her voice, telling him to keep praying, and the matter would be resolved.

Reginald stood and stretched. No matter what, the Lord would guide him and direct his path, just as his mother had always said. Although King Franklin seemed to think that Lorie was the perfect match for his son—which also meant she'd be the future Queen of Felinia—the fact remained that Reginald felt no love in his heart for her. None. And that troubled him greatly.

It suddenly hit him what he needed to do. What he *had* to do. He absolutely must have a heartfelt talk with his father. Just the two of them, without Wentworth being privy to the talk. Reginald left his office and walked slowly toward the king's private quarters, passing Genevieve in the hallway as he walked.

She paused and bowed. "Did you need anything, Your Highness?"

Reginald smiled and thanked her, replying he was going to see his father. He continued on down the carpeted hallway, passing the castle library on his right, where he caught a glimpse of Ludwig, one of the castle cats, lounging on a sofa. He couldn't suppress a grin. The castle cats seemed to prefer certain rooms, the library being one of them.

A few minutes later he reached his father's private quarters and knocked on the door. Wentworth answered, looking surprised to see Reginald. He bowed and stepped back, allowing the prince to enter, then politely asked, "Shall I leave, Prince Reginald? If you have private matters to discuss, I'll step out."

"Um, yes, if you don't mind, Wentworth. Just a bit of family business, but it should not take long. Thank you." Reginald walked toward his father, who was seated in his usual large chair near a window. Wentworth exited the room, and silence hung in the air for only a moment.

"Have a seat, my son. What's on your mind?" King Franklin cast a curious look at him. "Wentworth and I were just going over the upcoming week's schedule, so you haven't interrupted anything. You always apologize when you enter and I'm speaking with our loyal assistant." The king leaned forward as if to show his son he had his complete attention.

Reginald wondered if he was making a mistake. A *major* mistake. His father liked to have things mapped out. He'd taken great pride in the fact that his son—the heir to the throne of Felinia—would be married in the near future, and then would take over as king not too long after that.

King Franklin had let it be clearly known that he didn't intend to reign until his death, but would be a retired king, as he liked to phrase it. Being an independent country, Felinia had its own set of governing rules, and nothing prohibited the king from stepping down early from the throne. Would Reginald's confession to his father cause an upheaval in the king's well-thought-out plans for the future? He drew in a deep breath before speaking.

"Father, my heart is burdened, and this is something I've been praying about." He paused, looking directly into his father's eyes to gauge his reaction. All he saw was concern and curiosity.

Reginald continued. "Because I'm betrothed to

Lorie, we should be planning our wedding soon. But…” Could he bring himself to say it? What if this announcement affected his father's health? Reginald wouldn't forgive himself.

Yet, could he forgive himself if he went through with a marriage that held no love? A marriage that was a huge mistake? That wouldn't help anyone, including the citizens of the island. They deserved a ruler who thought clearly and didn't make life-altering mistakes.

“Father, I'm having second thoughts.” Why were those few words so difficult to say?

A puzzled frown furrowed the king's brow. “Second thoughts, my son? About the timing or location of the wedding?”

Reginald's stomach tightened. It was obvious his father didn't understand what he was attempting to say. He would need to be blunt, as much as he hated doing so.

“Father, the truth is…I don't love Lorie. If she's to be my wife, not to mention the future Queen of Felinia, there should be love involved.” He paused and drew in a ragged breath. “I've prayed about this matter a lot. I've even written a list of traits I admire about Lorie. But I cannot deny the most important fact that there is no love in the relationship. None. I honestly don't know if she feels any love toward me, but most likely not. She's probably just excited about marrying into royalty.”

Had he gone too far in verbalizing his thoughts? Yet he was speaking to his father, so he needed to be completely transparent, as awkward as this topic was. This concerned not only Reginald's future, but the future of his country, as well.

King Franklin remained silent for a few moments, appearing deep in thought as he tapped on the walnut sidearm. He was no longer frowning, but now his eyes held sadness. "I see."

"I'm sorry, Father. I'm sure this news is upsetting to you." What else could Reginald say? Actually, he might prefer anger to the look of sadness on the king's face. He'd never wanted his father to be disappointed in him. And the silence was troubling.

Finally, after what seemed to be an hour but in actuality was no more than seconds, the king cleared his throat and gazed directly at his son. A weak smile formed although the glimmer of sadness remained in his gaze. He placed his arms on the desk in front of him.

"No need to apologize, my son. I really should not be surprised, as the betrothal was more my doing than yours. I'm just heavily burdened that you were going to marry someone for whom you feel no love."

Reginald's heart lifted. Was his father going to permit him to get out of this betrothal?

The king lowered his eyes. When he returned his gaze to Reginald, he spoke calmly with no hint of judgment in his tone. "I'm glad you came to me about this matter. A major decision that will affect not only you and Miss DeVenes, but also many others as well." He lifted a nearby cup of tea to his lips. After a sip, the king replaced the teacup and returned his gaze to his son's face.

"Now, what we must do, Reginald, is decide the best way to proceed with this information." He steepled his fingers in front of him. For a few seconds his mouth seemed to be set in a grim line, but then a slight grin formed, surprising Reginald.

"First and foremost, I must say I am proud of you, son. I know this wasn't easy to tell me. We don't want to make a hasty decision and end up having regrets, so I suggest you and I both pray about this situation for the next few days. Then we will decide how to handle talking with the DeVenes family. Of course, you'll need to speak to Miss DeVenes privately to spare her humiliation in front of her parents."

"Thank you, Father. I cannot tell you how relieved I am that you understand my feelings. And no, I certainly don't want to humiliate Lorie or handle this hastily, so I will continue praying." Reginald had the sudden urge to rush over and hug his father, but that might be a bit much. As kind-hearted as the king was, he was never one to display affection.

"Now…I suppose we need to inform Wentworth and make certain he doesn't breathe a word of this to anyone." The king gestured to the door, so Reginald stepped over and swung it open, almost expecting to see the man with his ear up to the door. Thankfully, the loyal assistant was standing a few feet away, as if guarding the king's office without standing too close.

After Wentworth entered, the door closing behind him, the king proceeded to inform him of the news. Reginald had to work hard to keep from laughing, because it was obvious the news shocked him. In fact, Reginald didn't recall ever seeing the assistant with such widened eyes.

"I see, Sire. Very well, you can trust me completely to keep quiet about this matter. Whenever I do need to contact anyone or if there's anything I need to do, please notify me and I will handle it." With his hands clasped behind his back and his expression stoic, Wentworth presented the picture of a truly loyal assistant to the royal family.

"Thank you, Wentworth. Prince Reginald and I felt certain we could trust you, otherwise we would have withheld this most important news. Although it seems rather unfortunate, I feel certain that one day we shall look back and see that this was for the best."

Minutes later as Reginald returned to his office, he felt as though a weight had been lifted from his shoulders. His father's reaction to the news of his feelings—or lack thereof—for Lorie was far better than he'd anticipated. His father genuinely must have picked up on the fact that Reginald didn't feel any love toward the young woman, no matter how impressive her family background might be.

He uttered a silent prayer of thanks for his father's understanding and acceptance. Then he offered another prayer that the Lord would guide and direct him toward the right woman for him. One he would truly love.

~ ~ ~

Was she really doing this? Tina's hands shook as she clasped the ticket printed out for her by the kind hotel clerk before she departed Rome that morning. The shuttle ride from the hotel to the Rome airport seemed a blur, even though she was trying to absorb all the sights she could before leaving this wonderful country.

Another American passenger in the shuttle with her smiled and inquired, "Where are you from?" The middle-aged man appeared to be a businessman from his suit, tie, and briefcase.

She cleared her throat. "Tennessee. But I'm

headed to Felinia." Why couldn't she state it in a matter-of-fact tone? After all, she wasn't doing anything wrong. People changed their travel plans all the time. *But not me. I'm a small-town girl who's on her dream trip, and now I should be heading home.* Tina attempted to ignore the chiding voice in her head.

Her fellow passenger's face brightened. "Ah, Felinia. The tiny island country with the big heart." He chuckled at her surprised expression. "Yes, that's supposedly their motto, I've heard. And the one time I visited there it suits the island well. It's tiny, that's for sure. And everyone I encountered seemed as friendly as they could be." He paused and eyed her curiously. "Have you been there before?"

She briefly explained the emergency landing her plane made while enroute to Italy, noting the man's startled expression.

"In all my years of flying for business trips, that's never happened. I'm sure that was terribly frightening." He seemed interested to learn what happened.

Tina nodded and admitted it was scary, but everyone was fine. She added that the Felinia airport staff had shown gracious hospitality to the unexpected arrivals in their lobby. She made sure to omit details of meeting the prince, but she did mention his welcome speech to the group of passengers in the lobby.

The man nodded. "Yes, I've heard King Franklin and his son Prince Reginald are good men. No scandals or scuttlebutt on that pair, which is rare in this day and age." He chuckled again before adding with a playful arch to his eyebrows. "I've also heard that the prince is supposed to marry a young woman from Italy, but I'm not sure when. What a wedding that will be—I'm sure even the American papers and news stations will want to get a closer look at that major event."

He unbuckled his seat belt as the shuttle pulled up to the curb at the airport. "Well, safe travels to you, Miss. Enjoy your time in Felinia." The man gestured for her to exit the shuttle before him, a courtesy that Tina appreciated.

To Tina's great relief, she was able to locate the boarding area for flights to Felinia, and noted with amusement that there were only a handful of other passengers waiting in the small seating section. Was she doing the right thing? The question again taunted her, but she'd been praying diligently about this decision ever since the hotel clerk had offered information on flying to Felinia.

After the flight began, Tina sipped a cup of coffee and wondered if there was any chance she'd see the prince again, but knew it was highly unlikely. After all, the royal family surely didn't roam the island streets mingling with the residents. A royal family certainly must have their protocol.

And there was no sense in daydreaming about him, because he's betrothed. *And news flash—I'm not royalty, remember?* She'd have to treasure the memory of her time encountering him in the Felinia airport. That experience still seemed surreal to her.

The plane landed smoothly after which the passengers prepared to disembark. Suddenly a wave of panic washed over Tina. This was more than just a racing pulse or nervousness. *Pray.* The silent reminder whispered in her mind, so she asked the Lord to be with her in this foreign country. He'd kept her safe while in Italy, so the Lord would also be with her on this tiny island.

As she headed to the baggage claim area of the small airport, Tina took slow, deep breaths and willed herself to remain calm. She should be thrilled to have the opportunity for this bonus visit while on her trip. Besides, Lucy would be happy for her and want to hear all the details.

Getting her baggage only took about ten minutes, then she headed to the shuttle for the nearby hotel. She realized this bonus visit might not have been possible if not for the kindness of the helpful hotel clerk in Rome. He'd taken care of helping her with these arrangements, so she had the security of a hotel room awaiting her here in Felinia.

But as she went through the motions of her arrival on this island, at the back of Tina's mind remained one important thought that refused to leave her. Would she see the prince again? For all she knew, he might be away on a trip, representing his country somewhere or attending meetings. Besides, she knew basically nothing about the duties of a prince, even one of such a tiny country.

"Miss, are you ready to leave?" The shuttle driver spoke politely as Tina stood on the sidewalk, her mind lost in her own thoughts.

Only a few minutes later the shuttle arrived at the Felinia Hotel, a three-story structure that appeared old but well-maintained. The stone building had bright green double wooden doors, one of the country's main colors. Large stone lions posed on either side of the entranceway, and a burgundy-colored carpet covered a large area of the space in front of the doors. A matching awning hung over the entrance, to offer a bit of shelter for guests in the event of rain.

Tina and the other passengers climbed from the shuttle van, and after obtaining their bags and tipping the driver, the group headed toward the hotel door together. A hotel employee greeted them at the door.

"Welcome, friends. We are glad you are staying with us and want you to have an enjoyable visit while you're visiting our beautiful island." The man, who appeared to be in his mid-fifties, offered a warm smile underneath a dark brown moustache. "I am Giovanni, your host today at the Felinia Hotel. Now, if you will step to the counter, we will assist you as quickly as possible." He lifted a hand and snapped his fingers, summoning the attention of two young men working behind the hotel counter.

It didn't take long before Tina headed to the elevator, room key in hand. She glanced around at the clean interior, noting the touches of Mediterranean décor surrounding them. Live green plants lined the wall every few feet, creating a jungle-type feel in the lobby and elevator area.

Minutes later, Tina was on the second floor, unlocking the door to her room. She was pleased with what awaited her—a large bed with a beautiful, floral-print spread and decorative pillows, older but lovely furniture, and a vase of fresh flowers on a small round table next to the window. Right away, she knew she'd enjoy her stay here, although it would be brief.

She sent text messages to her brother and Lucy, giving them quick updates so they'd know where she was and that she was safe. Taking out her small travel planner, she made a quick list of places she'd seen on the Felinia website. As she jotted notes, an image of the handsome prince hovered in her thoughts. The chances of seeing him again were likely zero, not to mention that he'd probably not remember her anyway.

Closing her small travel planner, Tina stood and stretched. Tiredness was catching up with her. Even her body was a bit achy and her head was starting to throb. She'd take a headache tablet, rest for a few minutes, and then venture outside to look around while it was still daylight. She'd need something to eat, too, so hopefully there would be a café nearby.

After swallowing the tablet with a few sips of the bottled water she'd brought with her, Tina collapsed on the soft bed, savoring the comfort of the fresh, crisp sheets. Her tired body gave in to slumber, and when she awakened, she looked at her cell phone and gasped.

~ ~ ~

Why had she slept so long? Tina had only intended to take a cat nap—just enough sleep to refresh her body so she could begin sightseeing. Instead, she'd slept over two hours. And to her dismay, the achiness had spread to her torso and legs. She must've aggravated a muscle while pulling her luggage and carrying her heavy handbag.

Shoving away thoughts of her bodily aches, Tina pushed to her feet. At least she could step outside of her hotel for a glimpse of Felinia. After all, the hotel was in a different area than she'd been in at the airport, and she wanted to see all the sights she could. She also wanted to inquire about tours of the castle, although she hadn't read any information that those were offered. Well, a girl could dream.

Stopping at the hotel counter, Tina was relieved

when the clerk didn't seem surprised by her question, although his reply was disappointing. "No, I'm sorry but there are no castle tours open to the public. You are not the first visitor who has inquired about castle tours. Unfortunately, due to security concerns, the advisors to the royal family do not feel that would be a good idea. Thankfully, Felinia hasn't had any major issues with security, but hearing what has happened in some other countries is frightening, to say the least."

He looked genuinely remorseful, but then brightened as he described points of interest on a small map. A few minutes later, another guest stood behind Tina, waiting to speak with the clerk, so he folded the map and handed it to her. Then, with a parting smile, he assured Tina that if she had more questions, he was at her service.

"Thank you so much. You've been a tremendous help." Tina nodded and scooted away from the counter to give the man behind her his turn with the clerk. She hoisted her handbag on her shoulder, kept the map clasped in her left hand, and exited the hotel. There should still be at least a couple of daylight hours remaining, so Tina decided to explore the area near the hotel.

If only her aches and pains would stop. Unfortunately, her headache had returned and the soreness in her body persisted. Maybe she just needed fresh air. Trying not to think about her discomfort, Tina smiled at passersby on the sidewalk. A pleasant breeze drifted in from the sea, and a few gulls glided overhead. What a difference from her hometown in Tennessee!

Continuing on down the street, she passed various shops and businesses, many of them closed now that it was suppertime. As if on cue, her stomach growled and she looked at the map again, seeing the eateries that the clerk had circled. According to the map, there should be a café nearby. Maybe a bowl of soup would help her feel better.

As she approached the small café ahead on her left, Tina inhaled the pleasing aromas. She wasn't sure if she smelled fish frying or perhaps beef simmering, but whatever it was, it appealed to her. Maybe she needed more than soup.

"Do you recommend anything?" Tina asked her server, who heartily recommended the fish sandwich. After placing her order, Tina sipped the refreshing cola the young man had brought her and looked over her map again.

Although hungry, she still wasn't able to eat very much. What was wrong with her? Had traveling so far from home made her physically sick? Maybe she'd gotten overly tired, and her body still needed more rest.

Trying not to think about her aches, Tina focused on the other diners in the small café. Two middle-aged women sat at the next table, and Tina couldn't help overhearing snippets of their conversation. Her ears perked up as she heard them mention the prince. She also heard the words *wedding* and *Lorie.* That made sense, of course, since Tina knew that Lorie was the woman he was supposed to marry.

Given her current physical state, Tina finished nibbling only a few bites before pushing her meal away. She paid the bill and headed back to her hotel. If only she had more energy, she'd explore until dusk. But there was no way, so she entered the hotel, making sure to greet the kind desk clerk.

In her room, she gave in and flopped onto the soft bed to rest—for the second time that day. But she made up her mind that tomorrow she'd start out early and explore the island from dawn to dusk. She'd make the most of her time on this tiny island, even if she didn't catch a glimpse of the handsome prince.

~ ~ ~

Chapter 4

A mixture of emotions battled inside Reginald that week. Overwhelming relief that his father understood that his marriage to Lorie could not take place, but also dread of having to break the news to her. Not to mention breaking the news to her parents. That would be awkward, to say the least. Yet it must be done.

Why allow a marriage to happen when it was a mistake? Not only would that be extremely foolish, but sinful. If Reginald went ahead with the marriage, he'd be deceiving Lorie, and that was wrong. Was he meant to remain single? After all, how many opportunities did a prince have to meet an appropriate young lady? He must keep praying and trust that the Lord was in control.

A tapping at his door startled him. "Come in, please." He turned his gaze toward the door as Wentworth hurried in, clipboard in hand. The man certainly took his job seriously, which was a good thing. However, his stern, businesslike demeanor almost made Reginald laugh, because Wentworth reminded him of a character from a children's book.

"Good day, Prince Reginald. I've been conferring with His Majesty, and he wants to arrange a meeting with Miss DeVenes' family as soon as possible. He will discuss the matter with you himself, but he asked if I would go ahead and mention this and see if you have a preference concerning how this is handled." Wentworth paused and cleared his throat.

"Would you prefer an evening dinner with the DeVenes family in attendance? Or perhaps something on a smaller scale, such as an informal meeting with the two families in the meeting room here in the castle? Wherever you are more comfortable, Sire, is what your father wishes." He finished his spiel, cleared his throat again, and waited for Reginald's response.

Reginald resisted the urge to inform Wentworth his preference would be to hire a trained carrier pigeon to fly to the DeVenes' estate in Italy, deliver a note informing them that the prince no longer wished to marry Miss DeVenes, and be done with the entire matter. Of course, that would be unacceptable, and the very mention of such—even in jest—might cause poor Wentworth to fall over in a faint.

"I'm thinking perhaps an intimate meeting of the two families might be best. Certainly, having coffee or tea and refreshments served, but a simple gathering to notify them of the change in upcoming plans might be best. No need to let them think that we're inviting them for a happy planning session for a wedding."

He paused to gauge Wentworth's reaction, and realized the man was scribbling notes on his clipboard. The assistant took his duties to heart, almost to the extreme at times. His father had often commented that they would never need to worry about Wentworth neglecting his royal duties.

A slight smile appeared on the older man's lips, and he gave a brisk nod. "Very well, Sire. I will share your thoughts with His Majesty." He turned to exit, but paused. "Also…I'd like you to know that I'm sorry this did not work out, Sire." Wentworth almost appeared to be grieving, as sadness shadowed his eyes.

Reginald was touched. Wentworth had just expressed compassion in his own stoic way. With a smile, he thanked the assistant warmly. "That means a lot, Wentworth. Thank you very much. But rest assured, I genuinely feel I'm doing the right thing for everyone involved, and I've prayed a lot about this matter. It's unfortunate, but in the long run, it's for the best."

Again, Wentworth nodded, then exited the room. Reginald stepped over to the large window and gazed out at the courtyard. Brightly-colored flowers bloomed and birds flew in and out of tree branches. All was well in the kingdom. Or at least it would be soon—just as soon as he and his father had their meeting with the DeVenes family. And the sooner Lorie knew she wouldn't be marrying into royalty after all, the better.

Suddenly feeling the need for some fresh air, Reginald left his office and strode down the carpeted hall toward the elevator. He often smiled as he thought about the old castle having an elevator, yet it had been a welcome addition, according to his father, when it was installed many years ago.

A maid carrying a feather duster approached him and slowed her steps, then bowed slightly when she was a few feet from him. "Is there anything you need, Your

Highness?" She now held the feather duster behind her back, as if the sight of it might not be pleasant to the prince.

He smiled at her. "Thank you, Geneveive, but I am fine. Just stepping out for a bit of fresh air."

She nodded. "Very good, Sire." The maid continued along the hallway, her steps muffled in the thick carpet.

Minutes later Prince Reginald was in one of the castle courtyards, breathing in the early summer air and enjoying the birds' songs. This particular courtyard was on the front side of the castle, and although he was hidden from view to anyone who might be passing by the castle, as a child, he'd learned he could part branches of the hedge and peek between the iron gate if he chose. He'd done this before, when tourists were sightseeing on the road. However, today all was fairly quiet, with only the occasional vehicle driving slowly past.

He walked around the courtyard, trying to decide on his wording when he and his father met with Lorie and her parents. Oh, how he prayed his announcement wouldn't be too painful for his intended. After all, she really was a nice lady and he cared about her. Just not in the way he should care about the woman he was to marry. Not even close.

For some reason the image of the woman he'd met recently in the airport sprang to mind. *Tina*. Why did he continue thinking of her? He had relived that brief time with her over and over, recalling how she'd smiled while viewing the items in the memorabilia room. She'd seemed genuinely interested as he'd shared a small bit of his country's history. What a shame there had not been more time, because he loved sharing about his country and Tina had been an excellent listener.

"Sire?" A guard's voice disrupted his pleasant memories. Reginald turned and saw the uniformed man stepping toward him.

"Yes?" He hoped nothing was wrong, because he was enjoying this rather peaceful day.

The guard stepped toward him and bowed slightly from the waist. "Sire, you've been summoned to the king's office."

Reginald's pulse picked up. Was something wrong? What if his father was ill? Had the betrothal situation been too much for the older man?

~ ~ ~

Reginald thanked the guard and in record time reached his father's office. Relief swept over him as he entered and saw the king seated at his large mahogany desk, wearing a slight frown.

"Yes, Father? I was in the north courtyard and was told you wanted to speak with me. Are you feeling well?" He hoped his father wasn't having one of the bad headaches he suffered on occasion.

"I'm well, except for my concern about the upcoming meeting with the DeVenes family." He shook his head, stroked his whiskered chin, and continued speaking slowly.

"I have pondered exactly how we should present this change in plans to them and feel it wise for you to meet privately with Miss DeVenes first. After you've told her, then we can all meet and speak with her parents, expressing your change of heart as gently as possible. I do hope we can remain on amicable terms with the family. After all, we've been comrades for many years."

The king paused, took a sip of his tea, and continued. "Now remember, my son, I am in no way asking you to reconsider. If you've prayed earnestly about this matter and are certain you do not love Miss DeVenes, then you certainly should not marry her. I'm simply wanting this to go as smoothly as possible." The understanding in the king's gaze let Reginald know his father was still supportive of his decision to break off his betrothal to Lorie. And that was a huge relief.

His father's opinion meant the world to him. It always had. Not because the man was a king, but because Franklin was Reginald's father, and their relationship had become even stronger in recent years, with a special closeness since the passing of the queen.

"Thank you, Father. Your understanding and support mean a great deal to me. I've had no second thoughts about my decision, and the fact that I have prayed so earnestly about this and have peace assures me I'm doing the right thing. As much as I don't want to upset Lorie, I know it wouldn't be fair to either one of us to go through with marriage." He paused, unsure if he should even mention the other burden on his heart, but forged ahead.

"Father, something else that greatly concerns me is how this will affect your relationship with Lorie's father. I know you've not only been friends, but also have common financial interests." He tried to ignore the sick feeling in his gut. His decision to end the betrothal could have negative consequences for his father, something Reginald would never want to happen.

For a few moments the king didn't respond. Then

he slowly spoke as his gaze met his son's eyes. "My son, as much as this entire matter does trouble me for various reasons, my first and foremost concern is your happiness and well-being. Knowing now that you don't have deep feelings for Miss DeVenes, I would never, ever encourage you to proceed with marriage to her, no matter how this affects any friendships or financial concerns." The king paused and drew in a deep breath.

"Yes, it is true that her father and I have maintained a good friendship, and I would like that to continue. It is also true that he and I have discussed some common financial ventures, and to be quite honest, I was looking forward to working with him. However, I would be a heartless man if I put those concerns above the happiness of my very own son." Moisture pooled in the king's eyes.

Seeing his father and hearing the heartfelt words the man spoke brought tears to Reginald's eyes. He nodded, not trusting his voice at the moment. What on earth would Wentworth think if he entered the king's office and found them both in tears? That thought almost caused Reginald to laugh.

He stepped over to his father's desk and patted his arm. "Thank you, Father. Knowing how you feel means more than I can say." He paused, tamping down his emotions so as not to cause his father any greater concern. After all, the king was already dealing with enough. His only son's much-publicized betrothal was about to be called off. "Please know that I will handle this situation to the very best of my ability, and I will continue praying and seeking the Lord's guidance."

"I know you will, my son." The king sat up straighter, jutted his whiskered chin, and smiled. "Now, we need to get busy and plan when we are going to meet with the DeVenes family, so we can attend to other matters. After all, we have a country to look after." He offered a salute to his son, who returned the gesture as he stepped out to summon Wentworth. Not surprisingly, the loyal assistant stood in the hallway as though anticipating he would be needed.

Minutes later, the three men sat around the king's desk, discussing possible dates and the handling of such a delicate matter. When Reginald left his father's office twenty minutes later, he was drained. Yet, after hearing his father's heartfelt words, a ripple of genuine happiness surged through him. How could one man be filled with happiness and a strong sense of dread all at the same time?

Yet, no matter how Lorie and her parents accepted the news of the broken betrothal, the Lord would show him what he needed to do in the future. If he could only stop thinking about the beautiful woman named Tina.

~ ~ ~

Early the next morning, Tina awakened to the buzzing alarm clock on the bedside table in her hotel room. She shut if off then sat up. To her dismay, she still had body aches and a throbbing head. Maybe all she needed was coffee and a little breakfast, then a headache tablet if she wasn't feeling better.

An hour later she'd showered, drank some of the water she kept in her hotel room's small refrigerator, and nibbled a granola bar from her bag. Telling herself she'd feel much better after drinking some coffee, Tina grabbed her handbag and the map the hotel clerk had given her and she left her room.

Downstairs the familiar clerk greeted her with a smile, asking about her plans for the day.

"First, I'm going to get some coffee, then I plan to do some sightseeing. Thank you again for this map— such a big help for me."

The man graciously nodded and held up a finger. "We can fix some coffee for you here. No need to purchase any from a café." He scurried out from behind the counter and disappeared into a small room off of the lobby, appearing less than a minute later holding a Styrofoam cup with steam wafting from the top. "Here you are, Miss. I hope you will enjoy. Cream and sugar are on the small table." He gestured to a wooden side table bearing a vase of colorful flowers, surrounded by paper napkins, packets of sugar, and a small pitcher of cream.

"Thank you so much. All I need is cream in my coffee, and I'm all set." She grinned at the man, warmed by the kindness he'd shown.

"I hope you'll enjoy your day. If you use the map as a guide, you'll see there are several places nearby that are easily within walking distance. The shuttle stops are also located on the map if you prefer to take a ride to see more of our lovely island." At that moment another hotel guest approached the counter, so the clerk gave Tina a parting nod before turning his attention to an older woman waiting to speak with him.

Carefully holding the cup of aromatic coffee, Tina stepped out into the bright sunshine and drew in a deep breath. Surely after sipping the warm liquid and taking in some fresh island air she'd feel better. Regardless, she needed to make the most of her time and see as much as possible. She sat on a nearby bench and perused the map. Hmm…should she walk aimlessly along these nearby streets or plot out a specific course of action?

Still wishing that the castle offered tours, she suddenly had an idea. She would take a shuttle that passed by the castle, and that way she could at least have a better look at the beautiful old structure. *A beautiful old structure that houses a handsome young prince.* The thought popped uninvited into her mind, and she released a sigh. Maybe his wedding would be televised in the states so she could at least get another glimpse of him. And his bride.

Slowly standing, Tina headed to the nearest shuttle stop. She tossed her now-empty cup into a waste receptacle nearby, and then plopped onto a bench at the stop and waited. It was interesting to people-watch as she waited for the shuttle, and soon several others had joined her at the stop.

An older gentleman inclined his head toward her as they waited, then he inquired where she was heading.

"I'm hoping to get a look at the castle." She may as well be wearing a badge that stated she was a tourist, she mused.

The man's eyes crinkled at the corners. "Ah, yes. Our Felinia Castle is a sight to behold. When this shuttle heads south for several blocks, you'll be on the road. You can only get so close, since the land around it is guarded, of course. But the shuttle will slow its speed for anyone who wishes to snap a picture of the building."

"Thank you, sir. I appreciate your information. Are you a resident of Felinia?" As soon as the question left her mouth, Tina felt a bit foolish. Since the man had referred to the building as 'our castle,' surely he must live on the island. More evidence that she was a tourist.

However, the kindly man seemed happy to answer her question as he bobbed his head. "Yes, I'm very blessed to call this island my home now. For the past twenty years I've resided here, and now have no desire to live elsewhere." He paused as the sound of the approaching shuttle drew closer. "I enjoy riding the shuttle several blocks away, then walking back to my home here in the village. Keeps me young." He winked, then gestured for her to step onto the waiting shuttle ahead of him.

After the other passengers had already boarded the small vehicle, Tina dropped her money into the box beside the driver, thankful she'd had her payment ready and didn't have to dig for it in her bag. To her relief, the shuttle wasn't overly crowded or noisy, which might've made her headache worse.

The gentleman she'd been speaking with seated himself in front of her, and as the shuttle pulled away from the curb, he turned around and extended an aged hand. "My name is Enrico, and I've enjoyed talking with you."

Tina shook his hand and reciprocated his greeting. She wondered if he was a lonely widower, or perhaps his wife was busy doing other activities while Enrico got his daily exercise. He was a friendly man, but not pushy. A kind grandfatherly type.

On the shuttle's next two stops, more passengers climbed aboard, and on the third stop Enrico stood to disembark. "A pleasure meeting you, Tina. I do hope you'll enjoy your visit to our beautiful island." He smiled warmly at her before stepping off the shuttle to begin his walk back home.

She had to admire the man. He must be well into his seventies and was still intent on daily walking. With her recent aches, she figured the older man could likely outwalk her.

Tina returned her attention to the views out the window. So far, they'd passed a lot of foliage, some houses, and a few businesses. Now she was aware of murmurings around her on the shuttle, and the word *castle* caught her ears. The lady across from her looked out the window as she exclaimed, "I can't wait to get a look at this castle. I've heard it's lovely so I have my camera ready."

Tina nodded, then hastily dug into her handbag to pull out her camera. She could use the camera on her cell phone, but she might score a better shot using her trusty digital camera. Just then the shuttle driver's voice came over the speaker.

"Your attention please. For those interested, Felinia Castle is located ahead on the right. Although we are not permitted to get close, you can still enjoy a nice view as I pause at the curb. Please be ready with your cameras if you wish to take a photo, because I won't be able to stay at the curb long."

The voices around Tina grew more excited, yet there were a few on board who apparently were residents of the island, because they showed no interest at all. In fact, those passengers appeared a bit jaded at the excitement and comments of the others. Tina supposed that if a person lived close to something, it would lose its special appeal. But for her, the thought of seeing the Felinia Castle held much appeal. Especially since she knew who resided within the castle walls.

At the thought of Prince Reginald, her pulse quickened. Such a handsome, kind man. She would forever treasure the small amount of time she'd spent with him at the airport.

Tina could hardly contain her excitement as she caught her first glimpse of the magnificent building. It was truly a sight to behold. Not as large as some of the castles she'd read about in Europe, yet still spectacular. Made of stone with elaborate trim work around many of its windows and doors, there were two turrets on the front, with windows that sparkled as the morning sunlight shone on them. The castle maids must work very hard keeping everything shiny and bright.

But it wasn't only the building that was an amazing sight. The grounds that were visible to the public were quite beautiful. The manicured lawn displayed countless colorful blooms that seemed to be almost everywhere around the outside of the castle. From this distance, Tina couldn't be sure what types of flowers were blooming, but they appeared to be zinnias and roses in shades of red, pink, and purple, with an extra amount of yellow, most likely since that was a color in the flag of Felinia.

If only the passengers were allowed to step out of the shuttle for a couple of minutes. But the driver had again reminded everyone to take quick photos because he had to keep the shuttle moving along.

After she snapped five photos, the vehicle continued slowly down the road, and a twinge of disappointment filled her. She had a longing to see not only the prince again, but also more of the castle. Maybe all the fairy tales she'd read to her kindergarten students had become a bit too real to her, and she yearned to live one herself.

Tina decided to get off at a stop not too far from her hotel. She was ready to sightsee on foot now, although her achiness and headache pain persisted, no matter how much she ignored her symptoms.

When the woman across from Tina stood to get off at the next stop, the woman turned to her and spoke in a lowered tone. "I'm guessing you're a tourist like I am, so I'll share what someone told me. Be careful on the west side of the island, because that's a run-down area that's not considered safe." The woman smiled sadly and shook her head, then brightened and waved good-bye.

Tina appreciated the stranger giving her a heads-up, but she felt sad to think this beautiful island had such an area. She supposed no country was immune to poverty—even a country as beautiful as Felinia.

She continued absorbing all the sights out of her window, amazed at all the lush growth and greenery on this island—a true paradise. So far, she'd seen no indication of any area that appeared run-down.

Map in hand, Tina got off at the next stop, thanking the shuttle driver before stepping off. He seemed to appreciate her comment, because he smiled humbly and nodded. Standing on the sidewalk, Tina looked around at her surroundings. According to the map, she was only two blocks from her hotel, so she'd just walk slowly, enjoy the sights, and try to ignore the fact she wasn't feeling any better.

Hopefully she hadn't picked up a virus, because by now she should be feeling better. Refusing to give in to her aches, she focused on the sights around her. Even with light traffic on the streets, Tina could easily hear birdsong from nearby trees. A steady breeze from the sea blew in.

When she'd taken only a few steps, a thought formed and on impulse she acted on it. Turning around, she began to walk back toward the castle. After all, the shuttle had driven on that stretch of road, so why couldn't a pedestrian walk along there? She did remember seeing two men she assumed were guards standing by the wrought iron gates, but what could they do to her? Nothing except to tell her to keep moving, or that there was no foot traffic permitted in that area.

Hoisting her handbag higher on her shoulder, Tina walked along, determined to make the most of her brief visit on this beautiful island. Lugging her handbag everywhere didn't help her aches, but she had no choice. Passing other pedestrians now and then, she smiled as they made eye contact, and most of them appeared friendly, even uttering greetings to her. Cats lounged in the sunshine or perched on windowsills.

Was she headed in the right direction? Surely this was the same road the shuttle had traveled on, wasn't it? Each step seemed to be harder, and she had the urge to stop and sit in the grass. But she needed to keep moving.

Tina finally spotted the castle ahead, which filled her with a huge sense of relief. She would snap a few more photos, take in as much as she could, then turn around and head back to her hotel. Although on second thought, she may just catch a shuttle for the return trip. By now she honestly didn't think she could walk all the way back on foot.

Thankfully, there were a few other pedestrians along the side of the road, but apparently, they knew they were not supposed to linger because they all kept a brisk pace. Or perhaps they were local island residents and had seen the castle so many times that it wasn't anything spectacular to them.

After she snapped a few photos, an overwhelming exhaustion claimed her. She needed to sit for a few minutes, but what if a guard scolded her? Keeping her gaze focused on the castle, she tried her best to think only about the beauty of the stone exterior. What would it be like to have a peek inside those walls, or to stroll around the castle grounds? The thoughts bounced around in her tired brain. Why was she so tired?

Suddenly Tina's vision grew dark, even though she knew the sun was still shining brightly. The castle seemed to be spinning. What was happening? She approached a guard…maybe he had a bench where she could sit. She was so very tired. Tina tried to speak to the guard…then everything went black.

~ ~ ~

"What is it, Hilda?" The castle maid had stopped Reginald in the corridor. But it was her wide eyes and high-pitched voice that caught his attention.

"I beg your pardon, Your Highness, but I've just witnessed someone falling over onto a guard out front. I was going about my duties in the front parlor and glanced out the window to see a woman. She fell right over, Sire." Now Hilda was wringing her hands.

Surely this was not some kind of attack on the castle? Had someone used a woman to distract one of their guards while others gained entrance inside the castle grounds? He hoped and prayed that was not the case, yet he'd been instructed that in the current times, sadly, the royal family had to be prepared for unseen threats.

"Have you alerted anyone else, Hilda?"

The maid shook her head, still wringing her hands. "You're the first person I came upon, and knew you'd want to know."

Certainly the guard would have radioed inside for help by this point. Or maybe it was just a wayward tourist who'd lost her way or tripped and fallen. Perhaps an elderly woman lost her footing. After all, Hilda hadn't specified the age of the woman.

He thanked the maid and assured her he would check into it immediately. Hurrying toward the front parlor to see for himself, Reginald reached the room seconds later and saw one of the guards assisting a woman over to the iron gate, apparently to prop her against it since there was nowhere to sit on the outside portion of the partition.

Craning his neck for a closer look, he could tell the woman had auburn hair, which shone in the early summer sunshine. Maybe she'd only become overheated and had fainted. Reginald hoped it was nothing serious, but he didn't suspect any kind of terroristic activity from the scene he observed at the moment. He also didn't see anyone else around. The woman had been lowered to the ground by the guard, so at least she'd not fallen onto the concrete. The other guard remained at his spot.

Just as he was wondering if the guard had called for assistance on his radio, two workers rushed out to help. To Reginald's surprise, he saw one was Wentworth, no doubt wanting to see for himself what was going on. Behind him scurried Mrs. Bell, from the kitchen. She carried a cloth, which she promptly placed on the woman's forehead after kneeling over the woman.

Reginald had no doubt their trustworthy castle staff would handle the matter. As he watched, he saw the woman moving her head and hands as she patted Mrs. Bell's arm, as though in a gesture of appreciation. When the woman turned her head to the side, Reginald gasped. Could it be?

He leaned closer to the window, focusing his gaze on the woman's face. Yes, there was no mistaking this was the same woman he'd encountered in the airport. The American woman named Tina. Had Wentworth realized who she was?

Without giving the matter another thought, Reginald rushed toward the nearest side door that would allow him to exit the castle and approach the small group out front. Wentworth might not approve of the prince stepping outside unannounced, but so be it. He wanted to assure himself the woman was okay. *Be honest, Reggie. You want to see her close-up again.*

Stepping out the side door, Reginald strode toward the group but remained inside the wrought iron gate. "Is everything okay, Wentworth?"

At the sound of the prince's voice, Wentworth whipped his head around and looked startled to see the prince. "Yes, Sire. No need for you to be troubled. Apparently, this young lady became overheated and must've fainted." He glanced back at the woman, a slight frown forming, then he returned his gaze to Reginald. "I'm sure she will be fine and on her way momentarily, Your Highness."

Reginald stepped closer to the gate, noticing that

she looked very pale. Did she even have the strength to stand on her own? It was doubtful she could even walk back to wherever she was staying in her weakened condition.

At the moment, he didn't care about royal protocol. Although still inside the gate, Reginald leaned onto the iron structure and spoke gently, "Hello. Are you feeling better?"

She was now sitting up, and slowly turned her head toward him. Her eyes held a mixture of embarrassment and fear. Did she think she was in trouble? She couldn't help that she'd fainted.

There was no doubt this was indeed the same woman he'd encountered in the airport and had proudly shown pictures to in the memorabilia room. *The same one I've thought of countless times since that day.* Reginald drew in a breath and attempted to remain composed.

"I-I am so sorry…I was taking a walk and must have fainted." Just speaking those few words seemed to exhaust her, and she obviously struggled to keep sitting up. "I'm sorry." She appeared apologetic and her hand was shaking as she smoothed back tendrils of hair.

"No need to apologize, Miss. Is anyone with you, that we might call to come and assist you?" As he watched his question register with the woman, he noted how frail she appeared. Reginald had the ridiculous urge to rush through the gate, take the woman into his arms, and assure her that she'd be fine. What was wrong with him?

When she slowly shook her head, Reginald knew he must do something to help her. She was obviously still shaken from the ordeal. There was no way he'd allow her to be left on the sidewalk while she regained her strength.

His mind racing, Reginald leaned closer toward Wentworth. "I know this is out of the ordinary, but I want this young lady brought inside the castle and made comfortable. She is unable to walk back to her hotel or wherever she is staying." He held the assistant's gaze as if silently reminding him that he was serious. And being the prince, his commands were to be obeyed, protocol or not.

"Yes, Your Highness." Wentworth spoke solemnly as he nodded. "I'm sure Mrs. Bell will assist the young lady." He looked at the head kitchen worker, who'd been kind and attentive to their unexpected visitor.

After exchanging a few brief words with the guard to make sure nothing else had occurred before he'd joined them by the fence, Reginald then turned back toward the castle to lead the way as Mrs. Bell escorted the woman and Wentworth followed. As his mind raced, Reginald was struck with the thought that perhaps the castle doctor should be summoned, but he wouldn't jump to conclusions.

Inside the castle corridor, Mrs. Bell helped the woman named Tina to a velvet chair. Reginald stepped closer to the chair. "I believe you're the lady I met at the airport. Is that correct?"

Her face turned crimson, and she nodded, eyes downcast. "Yes." Her reply came out softly.

"Tina. Is that correct?"

At hearing her name spoken by the prince, she jerked her head upward, though she blinked several times as if dizzy. Slowly nodding again, she offered a slight smile and replied, "Yes, Tina Ransom, from Tennessee." There was no doubt the poor woman was dazed.

"I wanted to make sure I remembered correctly." Reginald paused as he noticed Mrs. Bell's puzzled expression, so he offered a brief explanation of encountering Tina at the airport after the emergency landing of her plane.

As they continued standing clustered in the hallway, Wentworth leaned toward Reginald. "Your Highness, perhaps after the young lady feels better, we can send for transportation back to her hotel?"

"That's a good idea, Wentworth. Thank you. For now, we need to ensure that our guest gains her strength back. Mrs. Bell, would you please escort her into the front parlor and arrange for some refreshment?"

The plump cook nodded eagerly, as if thrilled to be entertaining a female guest at the castle—albeit an unexpected beauty.

As Tina shuffled along with Mrs. Bell to the parlor, Reginald leaned in to his assistant and spoke in a low voice, "I want to make absolutely certain the young lady is well enough to return to her hotel, Wentworth. So, I'll speak with her myself and see what I can learn."

At Wentworth's surprised expression, Reginald patted his arm. "No need to be concerned about the possibility of an enemy attack. I would stake my life on the fact that this woman is an innocent tourist and has no ties whatsoever to any terror groups."

After a slight hesitation, Wentworth responded, "Yes, Sire. Whatever you think is best. Shall I see the king and inquire as to his thoughts about this matter?"

Reginald shook his head with more vigor than

necessary. "No need to disturb my father. Thank you anyway, but I will handle this situation. The lady most likely became overheated. Once she's feeling better, we can arrange transportation as you suggested. But I would feel terrible taking a chance that she might head out and become sick while on the streets." Reginald was relieved that his assistant apparently agreed with him. Beneath that rigid, stoic demeanor, Wentworth was truly a caring man.

The two men walked along the carpeted hallway to the front parlor, where Mrs. Bell hovered over Tina like a mother hen. Another maid had brought in lemonade and cookies, served on delicate china and set on a small table to Tina's left side.

"Are you feeling better after some refreshment?" Reginald asked softly as he and Wentworth entered the parlor.

Tina looked up and nodded, still appearing weak as she held a teacup with shaking hands. "Y-Yes, thank you so much. I'm terribly sorry about the trouble I've caused." Her words mirrored the expression on her face.

Reginald was pleased to see Mrs. Bell pat her arm and console in a soft voice, "There, there dear. No need to apologize."

"Exactly, Mrs. Bell." Then, focusing on Tina, he added, "You cannot help that you became ill, and we hope the lemonade and cookies will give you some strength."

"Thank you again. This has helped me, and I should be able to return to my hotel." She started to stand but grabbed the nearest wall. Mrs. Bell immediately urged her to sit a while longer, assuring her that she was not causing any trouble.

Wentworth had left the parlor but returned to inform the prince he had to attend a meeting in ten minutes. Reginald thanked him before turning his attention to Mrs. Bell. He spoke softly to her, hoping his words didn't reach Tina's ears.

"When she feels strong enough, call for a shuttle for her and tell them I shall cover the expense. But I would like to request that she leave her hotel information with us so we can check on her well-being." He made sure to keep his tone businesslike and was relieved when Mrs. Bell didn't appear a bit surprised at his comments.

"Certainly, Your Highness. I will make certain to follow through with your request." She bowed slightly.

"I'm sorry to have to leave your company, but I've been summoned to a meeting. However, Mrs. Bell is going to look after you and make sure you have transportation back to your hotel. Please take care, Miss." Reginald held her gaze, feeling something running through him that he couldn't explain, a yearning to spend more time with her.

But how ridiculous! This was only the second time he'd been around this American woman and he knew absolutely nothing about her. He needed to focus on his royal duties and exit the parlor before he stood there gazing at her like a lovesick young boy.

"Thank you again for your kindness, Your Highness." Her words came out softly and her emerald green eyes glistened.

He nodded at her, then at Mrs. Bell before exiting the parlor. As Wentworth accompanied him down the hallway, Reginald couldn't deny the strong yearning to remain in the parlor with Tina. What was it about her that pulled at him so? Suddenly he was aware that Wentworth was eyeing him curiously.

"Your Highness, I must say your kindness to that young woman is certainly admirable. Especially since we know nothing about her. And how interesting that she's the same woman we encountered in the airport recently."

"I would be a tyrant if I'd treated her any differently, Wentworth. Showing courtesy to someone who's fainted in front of the castle grounds is the right thing to do. My mother—God rest her soul—taught me not only good manners but kindness for my fellow man. And woman." He added the last words hoping that his assistant had no idea of the effect Tina had on him.

"Yes, Sire. Your mother was a remarkable lady." Wentworth's tone had grown even more serious than usual.

The two men continued the walk in silence, reaching the king's office door a few minutes later. After they'd entered, King Franklin looked up with an almost-amused smile and questioned, "What's this I hear about a tourist becoming ill outside of the castle grounds?" He sat back in his large chair as if settling in to hear a story.

Reginald briefly explained that the woman had fainted while sightseeing, and one of the castle guards had assisted her. "It just so happens that the American lady is the same one Wentworth and I encountered at the airport recently." He then reminded his father of the emergency landing on their island only a few days earlier, and the woman he and Wentworth had seen in a hallway at the airport. "She seemed very nice and was quite interested in learning about Felinia, since her flight had an unexpected landing here.”

“You are certain she is without concern, Reginald? No possible ties to any terror groups trying to gain information on our small nation?” King Franklin’s brow furrowed.

Reginald almost laughed, but knew it would be disrespectful, especially with Wentworth present. “No, Father. I have the utmost confidence that this particular lady is simply an American tourist who was flying to Italy and had the misfortune of being on a jet that had engine trouble. When we encountered her in the airport hallway, she appeared embarrassed for being lost and not with the other passengers.”

“And the episode today was simply a matter of a tourist becoming overheated in our June sunshine. Not to mention she was on foot and we don’t know how far she’d walked. But Mrs. Bell is staying with her in the front parlor until she’s strong enough to leave, and she will arrange for a shuttle to transport her from the castle to her hotel. No need to be concerned, Father.”

Yet, as Reginald sat through the thirty-minute meeting with his father and their assistant, his mind kept drifting to Tina when he should’ve been focusing on the upcoming schedule being discussed. And *that* concerned Reginald—very much.

~ ~ ~

Chapter 5

Was she dreaming? Tina sat on a satiny-soft cushioned sofa in an extravagantly-furnished room called *the parlor* sipping lemonade from a beautiful china teacup. No, this was not a dream. She was, in fact, inside the Felinia Castle, being hovered over by a kind, middle-aged woman with a slight British accent named Mrs. Bell.

"What else may I get you, dear? More lemonade or shortbread cookies?" The plump lady gazed at her with compassion, as if sensing Tina's awkward embarrassment for what had happened.

"No, thank you, though. You've been so kind to me, and I really appreciate everything. I'm feeling much better now so I'm sure I will be fine to return to my hotel." She'd just finished her last bit of lemonade—possibly the best she'd ever had—and now looked up at the woman who remained by her side.

Mrs. Bell waved a hand and another worker scurried toward them. Tina heard Mrs. Bell say something to the younger woman about a shuttle, but she couldn't make out all of her words.

"If you are absolutely certain you're able to return to your hotel, a shuttle will be arriving soon. But the prince wishes for you to leave contact information with me so we can check on you. He has such a kind heart." She added the last comment with a grin.

The prince wanted her to leave contact information? For a few seconds her heart leaped for joy inside her, but then reality set in. Yes, most likely the castle staff would need to check on her and make certain she wasn't working for some spy agency. What a joke that would be for anyone who knew Tina Ransom.

But precautions were necessary. After all, this was a royal family of a small island nation. They had to protect themselves, and she was from another country. Not to mention the fact they knew nothing about her, other than her name and the fact she was from the United States.

Tina grabbed a sheet from a small notepad in her handbag and wrote her information, hoping it was legible. Normally, her penmanship was neat, but in her current shaky state, the writing wasn't her best.

After handing the paper to Mrs. Bell, Tina felt something brush against her leg. She looked down to see a beautiful, fluffy cat gazing up at her with curious green eyes. She reached to pet the cat's soft fur. Rumbling purrs came from the feline.

Mrs. Bell chuckled. "Ludwig, how kind of you to check on our visitor today." She gave the cat a gentle pat, then explained the royal family had two castle cats, Ludwig and Daisy. "You might have noticed our island has an abundance of felines." Her eyes twinkled. She was obviously a cat person, which made the woman seem even kinder.

"Ludwig is beautiful. I love cats, but my apartment doesn't allow pets, unfortunately."

The young maid who'd stepped into the parlor earlier returned to say the shuttle was approaching. With the maid on one side of her and Mrs. Bell on the other, Tina slowly left the parlor, walked down the carpeted hallway to the side door, and exited the castle. She still could not believe this was happening. A guard stood sentry at an iron gate, opening it to allow Tina to step outside the castle grounds.

Minutes later, Tina was on the shuttle after bidding goodbye to Mrs. Bell and the young maid, who both scurried back inside the castle once the shuttle pulled away. As she rode back to her hotel, Tina stared numbly out the window, trying to catch glimpses of the lovely island she'd yearned to see more of, had it not been for her illness.

Her body continued to ache, and her head still throbbed, so she knew the remainder of her brief visit here would be spent in her hotel bed, attempting to regain her strength for the return flight to America in just two days.

After collapsing between the fresh sheets on her soft hotel bed, Tina fell asleep quickly. However, when she awakened, a sense of gloom hung over her, despite vivid dreams of the handsome prince and the castle. She was quite certain she'd never see the man again.

But someday, when she felt better, she'd visit the island again. Maybe Lucy could accompany her and they'd tour Felinia together. Lucy would be enthralled at hearing her adventures, even though they'd only occurred due to Tina's fainting spell.

Two days later Tina pulled her luggage behind her as she stopped at the hotel desk to turn in her room key. She thanked the hotel clerk again for his kindness and helpful suggestions about sightseeing.

"Ah, Miss Tina. Surely you must visit Felinia again in the future when you are not ill. Then you can enjoy all the beauty our small island offers. I do hope you will have a safe, pleasant flight to your home in America." He reached out to squeeze her hand.

Tina fought a wave of melancholy washing over her. What was wrong with her? Surely her weakened state must be affecting her emotions. "Thank you, Giovanni. You've been so kind to me. Lord willing, I'll be able to return and visit one day in the future." If she didn't head to her waiting shuttle, she'd dissolve in a puddle of tears and cause the poor man alarm.

About ninety minutes later Tina gazed out the airplane window as the jet lifted off the runway at Felinia's small airport. Her heart caught in her throat as she gazed at the beauty below, and silently promised herself that if there was any way possible, she *would* return someday.

Although most likely she'd never again see the prince in person, she'd forever treasure her memories of the two times she was with him, brief though they were. His smile and good looks were only part of his charm, because his kind spirit toward Tina had made an impression on her she'd remember forever.

~ ~ ~

"Your Highness, are you feeling well? I do hope you've not contracted an illness from our unexpected castle visitor recently." Wentworth's voice held a mixture of concern and a tiny bit of feistiness. It was clear he hadn't been overly thrilled that the ill woman had entered the castle parlor.

Reginald forced a smile. "Yes, thank you Wentworth. I'm fine. And no, I'm certain I didn't pick up an illness from our guest. I'm just thankful one of our guards assisted her."

The truth was, Reginald had felt a bit out-of-sorts the past two days, knowing that Tina was returning to America. In fact, she very well could be flying to her home at this moment. At least he had her contact information in the United States, so perhaps he could correspond with her.

Aware of Wentworth staring at him, Reginald began talking about their current business. He'd allow himself to think about the beautiful woman from America later on, but for now he must focus on royal duties and not raise suspicion in his overly curious assistant.

"The meeting with the DeVenes family is scheduled, correct?"

"Yes, Your Highness. They will be joining us for an afternoon tea tomorrow. The king wants us to discuss how the matter will be handled. He wishes this meeting to be as smooth as possible. As I'm certain you do also, Sire." Wentworth's eyebrows furrowed, as if to communicate sympathy at the task awaiting him.

"Very well. We'll meet this afternoon and go over how Father and I will handle this. I'd appreciate your prayers, Wentworth. I never thought I'd have to do something like this." Indeed, never had Reginald dreamed he would find it necessary to end a betrothal, and while relieved that he had his father's support, he still felt a niggle of guilt and also some sadness.

Wentworth nodded. "Yes, Your Highness. I will be praying about this situation and am certain you and the king will handle it with the utmost decency." Genevieve appeared at the doorway just then, bowing and announcing that luncheon would be served in ten minutes.

"Thank you, Genevieve," Reginald responded before Wentworth had a chance to do so. He'd always tried to maintain a friendly relationship with the castle staff, while appreciating their respect in return.

That afternoon, Reginald was in his office trying to gather his thoughts about the upcoming meeting with the DeVenes family. He was due in his father's office in about thirty minutes, so he wanted to gather some ideas to present to his father. There was no easy way to go about this situation.

Stepping to a window that overlooked the small courtyard, Reginald lifted his gaze toward the sky, which was a brilliant blue on this early summer day. As he stared up at the sky, all he could think of was the fact that somewhere in that same sky at that same moment was a jet carrying a beautiful auburn-haired woman to America and out of his life.

The image of Tina refused to leave his mind. Even being so ill as she'd been after fainting, she still appeared lovely. But it wasn't only the loveliness of her creamy skin and emerald-green eyes that captured his attention. It was also her sweet spirit and gentle manner. And she was so sincere. He had no trouble imagining her with a classroom of young children.

It hit him that Lorie was also lovely and polite,

but she lacked the sincere gentleness and sweetness that Tina possessed. Although Reginald had only been around Tina twice, he was able to discern her genuine goodness in that short amount of time. Amazing. Not that he was intentionally comparing and contrasting the two women, but he couldn't help thinking about the stark difference in their demeanors. Lorie was the picture of polished propriety, while Tina was inquisitive, curious, and wonder shone in her eyes.

Glancing at his clock, Reginald mentally chided himself. He was supposed to be planning for the DeVenes meeting, not daydreaming about an American lady he barely knew. He sat at his desk and jotted down some thoughts to present to his father, hoping the king had better ideas. There was no way to avoid the fact that this awkward situation would hurt Lorie and her family. He prayed that she would be as relieved as he was to end the relationship now.

Minutes later, Wentworth appeared at his office door to escort him to the meeting with the king. The two men walked along in silence as Reginald's thoughts whirled. He absolutely *must* focus and save thoughts of Tina for later. His assistant was again staring at him.

"Are you certain you're well, Your Highness? Perhaps the royal doctor should be summoned."

Reginald suppressed a laugh and shook his head. "No need for that, but I do appreciate your concern. I assure you I am fine. To be honest, this current betrothal situation is weighing heavily on my mind. I'll be genuinely relieved when it's behind us."

"Yes, Sire. I understand and completely agree."

They'd reached the king's office to find King Franklin standing by a picture window overlooking his small private courtyard, hands clasped behind his back.

"Have a seat, men." He offered a somewhat shaky smile at his son and assistant as he ambled over to the mahogany desk. The king lowered his frame into the leather chair and settled back, steepling his fingers as he gazed across the desk. "Wentworth, even though you will not be in attendance tomorrow at our tea with the DeVenes family, I value your opinion. So whatever insight you may have on this situation would be appreciated."

Reginald nodded at his father's words, while also wondering if the stoic Wentworth had ever come close to ending a romantic relationship. Not that his own relationship with Lorie held any romance, because it didn't. In truth, it had been more of a way to merge the two families and combine common financial endeavors.

Wentworth appeared delighted by the king's words, as he nodded. "I appreciate your confidence in me, Your Majesty. I must be quite open in stating that matters of the heart are not my expertise; however, I will assist you and Prince Reginald however I can." A blush crept up the middle-aged man's face and he glanced away, showing a bit of embarrassment at the subject.

The king cleared his throat and gestured toward a notepad on his desk. "I've made some notes which I'll share. Reginald, then you may offer your thoughts and input."

The men sat around the king's desk and talked for a half-hour, finally deciding on the least awkward manner in which to break the news to Lorie and her parents. Now more than ever, Reginald knew he'd be greatly relieved when this so-called afternoon tea with the DeVenes family was behind him. What concerned him the most—even more than fretting about Lorie's feelings—was the impact this might have on his father. He'd have to continue praying that his words would be well-received, and the tea would go as smoothly as possible.

As Reginald was about to exit his father's office, King Franklin cleared his throat and asked a question that caused the prince to freeze. "Son, have you heard any news on the young woman?"

Reginald whirled around, hoping his face conveyed confusion even though he had a good idea of whom his father was referring. "The young woman?" He retraced his steps toward his father's desk. Wentworth stood, his impassive gaze focused on some papers on the desk.

The king nodded as the hint of a smile played on his lips. "Yes, the young woman who fainted recently. Surely you remember? One of our guards assisted her and even brought her into the castle." An arched eyebrow almost suggested his father might be jesting with him, although as sick as Tina had been it was nothing to joke about. But his father didn't realize how ill she'd been.

"No, Father. I'm assuming she flew back to America. Mrs. Bell took excellent care of the young lady while she was here. But I will say that from seeing her briefly, I could tell she was truly sick. Apparently, some kind of virus had caused her to be in a weakened state, besides walking in our island heat while sightseeing. It must've been too much for her. I'm thankful one of our guards and Mrs. Bell offered assistance to her." He abruptly stopped speaking, not wanting to sound as though he had any interest in the unexpected guest.

After his father nodded and spoke a few words about hoping the woman was okay and had a safe trip to America, Reginald left his office. Out in the carpeted hallway, he paused to collect his thoughts. Could his father possibly have discerned that his son had feelings for an American woman that he barely knew? Maybe he was being a bit paranoid. Still, he'd need to be careful not to let *anyone* know how drawn he'd been to Tina Ransom. After all, he still knew very little about her. Yet given the chance, he'd very much like to know more.

~ ~ ~

The dreaded day had come. Reginald read and re-read his morning devotions, praying that the Lord would guide his words and help the meeting with the DeVenes family go as smoothly as possible. Yet his pulse pounded faster as the day went on. He'd finished his breakfast in the privacy of his office. Soon enough he would be with other people when the three o'clock hour arrived, and the tea began.

Trying to do a few routine tasks at his desk was useless. He couldn't concentrate on anything because all he thought of was Miss Lorie DeVenes, who thought she was engaged to Prince Reginald but would soon learn the betrothal was off. How would she take the news? Would she ever forgive him for breaking it off?

Without giving it much thought, Reginald slid open a bottom drawer of his desk and lifted out a small photo album. What treasures the album contained, including some photos of his late mother and childhood memories. As he leafed through the pages, he stopped when he came to a page containing photos from a royal ball when he and Lorie had announced their engagement. A happy occasion, or so he'd thought at the time.

But had he been genuinely happy then, or simply going through the motions because that's what was expected of him? His fingers sifted through pictures of the elegant ball to celebrate their betrothal with many well-wishers in attendance. How festive it had all been. And now those people would be learning that there would be no royal wedding. At least not between Prince Reginald and Miss Lorie DeVenes.

About to close the photo album, Reginald's eyes fell upon another photo of Lorie and himself. She had a smile pasted on her face, yet it didn't appear sincere. He wasn't even smiling at all in this particular photo. Well, there you have it. That's what their relationship really consisted of—a man and woman who truly didn't love each other, yet were planning a marriage because that's what was expected.

Besides, how many times had the couple done any activities together, aside from events that both families participated in? Had there been any romantic dates with only the two of them? No, and Reginald had never had the yearning to be alone with Lorie, and apparently, she felt the same way. They were simply going through the motions. What a sad way to begin a lifelong relationship.

A tapping at his door snapped him from his thoughts, and Reginald called out for his assistant to enter. He'd learned long ago to recognize Wentworth's taps at his door so he always knew it was him. Sure enough, the middle-aged man entered the room, looking as though he was headed to a funeral.

"I'm ready, Wentworth. Thank you again for all of your help with this event." He felt foolish referring to this particular afternoon tea as an *event*, since the purpose would be to accomplish a most unpleasant task.

"I'm always honored to help, Your Highness." Wentworth's normally serious tone was even more dismal than usual, and he knew the assistant would be almost as relieved as he was to have this matter done.

When they entered the dining room, King Franklin was pacing around one end of the cherrywood table that was covered with an elegant white damask cloth. For a split second, Reginald had a flashback to his childhood years, when he had played underneath this very table and pretended to build kingdoms with his toy blocks. Such innocence of simpler times. There were days he'd like to snap his fingers and be that little boy again, playing to his heart's content underneath the table.

"Greetings, Father. Are you feeling well?" He eyed his father as the man slowed his pacing.

"Yes, I arrived a bit early and didn't want to sit, so I've been stretching my legs. Keeps my arthritis from getting the best of me." He chuckled, although it sounded forced.

Hilda appeared at the doorway to inform them the DeVenes had arrived. "Shall Genevieve escort them to this room, Your Majesty?" The petite maid bowed slightly as she asked the question.

"Certainly, Hilda. Wentworth, I do appreciate you making certain the kitchen staff has everything under control."

"Yes, Your Majesty. I checked on them earlier and everything was set to be served, but I shall make certain there are no problems. And I will continue praying this meeting goes well." Wentworth's eyes held compassion, and Reginald felt a sudden wave of emotion. He needed to steel himself, because he had to be strong for his father's sake.

As the DeVenes family was escorted to the dining room, Reginald greeted them at the doorway, then asked if he might speak privately with Lorie before they began tea. Curiosity shone on their faces as they nodded. He motioned for Lorie to step into the nearby parlor as he sent up a swift, silent prayer for the right words.

Looking directly into Lorie's eyes, he offered a sad smile before saying the words he'd dreaded, gently explaining that he must call off their betrothal. Then he added, "I'm so sorry, but after much prayer and soul-searching, I know it's for the best—for both of us." When she remained silent, Reginald went on. "You deserve someone who loves you dearly, not simply a marriage to unite two families."

An uncommon smirk replaced her polite smile. "I shouldn't be surprised, because we haven't spent much time together." Lorie's eyes pooled with moisture, and she released a bitter laugh. "You've barely kissed me." Her voice had taken on a shrill tone, and her hands trembled. Reginald hoped she wasn't going to become hysterical. To his relief, she didn't say more, although a few tears trickled down her face.

"I suppose we should join the others in the dining room. My father was going to explain the situation to your parents." Could this be any more awkward?

Reginald only hoped when his father broke the news to Lorie's parents, they handled it without drama.

The pair entered the dining room, where a heavy silence greeted them, along with three somber faces. King Franklin sent an apologetic look to his son, and a very discreet nod, letting him know the news had been delivered.

Mrs. DeVenes' eyes avoided his until her daughter was seated, then she reached over and patted Lorie's arm. Quietly, she said, "It will be fine, dear. Some things are just not meant to be." Then the middle-aged woman sniffed, keeping her eyes lowered.

Lorie's father at least looked at Reginald, but his lips tightened into a straight line.

Wentworth stood at the dining room doorway, and upon the king's signal, he alerted the maids that the group was ready for tea. Genevieve and Hilda silently entered, serving the guests tea, petit sandwiches, and delectable cookies. Under different circumstances, the table would appear to be a festive gathering, complete with a colorful vase of flowers in the center.

As the group began to eat and sip tea in silence, King Franklin cleared his throat, apparently determined to make the most of the event. "How has your weather been in Italy in recent days?"

Mr. DeVenes offered a brief reply, then resumed eating in silence, the air weighty with tension.

Reginald could barely consume a tiny chicken salad sandwich, followed by a sip of tea. His insides were in knots. He'd hoped that Lorie's parents and his father could at least have a somewhat polite conversation, but that was obviously not the case.

When everyone was finished, King Franklin

thanked their guests for coming, adding that he deeply regretted the reason for the visit. With a forced smile, he inquired, "Will you be staying on our island for a while, or do you plan to return to Italy?"

Mr. DeVenes replied stiffly, "We'll be returning to our home promptly. Our private plane is waiting at your airport, and the shuttle we hired is parked outside your castle grounds. Thank you for the refreshments, although the news has been quite unsettling, as you can imagine."

Reginald cleared his throat and stepped closer to Lorie's father. "I'm so sorry, Mr. DeVenes. As painful as this is, I didn't want to go through with a wedding and then realize we'd made a mistake." Reginald winced, knowing there was nothing else he could say or do.

Surprisingly, Lorie's father managed a sad smile and nodded. "We only want the best for our daughter and would never encourage a marriage if the prospective groom was not fully committed."

Wentworth stood at the dining room doorway to escort the guests out, being as gracious and polite as possible to the serious group. Lorie had gotten control of herself and now only sniffled as her mother stayed by her side.

Once the guests had left, King Franklin told his son they'd discuss things later, but he needed an afternoon rest. Wentworth escorted the king to his private quarters after quietly assuring Reginald he'd make sure the king wasn't feeling ill.

Reginald decided some fresh air might be good, so he headed to the small courtyard on the west side of the castle, relishing the breeze and chirping birds. How could he be so totally drained yet overcome with relief at the same time?

~ ~ ~

Later that afternoon, Reginald, his father, and their assistant gathered in the king's office. The king stroked his whiskers and looked at Reginald. "I do think some of her tears were from sadness at not becoming part of a royal family. However, it appeared to me that she might've also cried some tears due to embarrassment in front of her parents. Perhaps knowing they would be disappointed that their daughter was no longer marrying a prince."

The king then released a long sigh before continuing, "Regardless of how Miss DeVenes handles this matter in the days to come, you've done the right thing, my son. And I'm proud of you." His voice was thick with emotion.

A lump formed in Reginald's throat at his father's admission, and he also noticed that even Wentworth was dabbing at his eyes. Would wonders never cease? The composed assistant showing emotion was surprising, indeed.

"Thank you, Father. That means a great deal to me. I will continue praying that Miss DeVenes will accept the news of our betrothal without rancor and she'll move on with her life. I will also pray that your friendship with Mr. DeVenes will not suffer because of my decision."

King Franklin lifted a finger, now slightly bent with arthritis. "Now Reginald, as I've told you before, your happiness and well-being come far above my relationships—whether it's friendship or business." The hint of a smile played on the king's lips.

Wentworth cleared his throat. "I'm happy to know this meeting is behind you, Your Majesty. For both you and Prince Reginald. How shall we go about informing the castle staff? They are curious, as you might imagine. Especially after seeing Miss DeVenes with tears and her mother offering comfort as they exited the castle." A slight shake of his head implied that he felt Lorie's display was somewhat of an act.

"Wentworth, since we trust you, would you mind handling this task for us? Perhaps hold a staff meeting tomorrow morning and briefly explain that Prince Reginald is no longer betrothed to Miss DeVenes." The king paused and then frowned slightly.

A slight tone of harshness laced his next words. "And please inform our staff to refrain from speculation or false rumors. We don't need the gossip mill being tossed about throughout our island."

"Yes, Your Majesty. I will certainly follow through with this and make certain the staff understands." Wentworth held his head high, no doubt feeling pride at his service to the royal family. The man might take his duties a bit too seriously at times, but he was loyal and dependable to a fault, and that mattered a lot.

That evening Reginald sat in his private quarters, trying to read but failing to concentrate. He finally closed the book and placed it on his bedside table. He'd not eaten an evening meal, telling the kitchen maid who'd appeared at his door that he wasn't hungry due to the afternoon tea.

Although that was partially true, he doubted he would've been able to eat much of anything due to his current emotional state. Great relief was tinged with a bit of sadness at his broken betrothal. He'd never imagined he would have to do something of that nature, yet there was no doubt he'd done the right thing—for *all* concerned.

But above all of those thoughts, the image of Tina appeared in his thoughts, and he found himself wishing she was still visiting Felinia, rather than having returned to America. Yearning for her seemed to cause the most sadness of all, and that concerned him greatly.

~ ~ ~

Chapter 6

The heat of early summer wrapped its welcoming arms around Tina as she walked to her mailbox a few days after returning home from her trip. Although still a bit weak, she was feeling stronger and more like her usual self.

She'd been happy to see her hometown of Blueberry Cove, yet couldn't deny missing the lush beauty of Felinia. Not to mention seeing all the cats! Tina couldn't wait to share photos and all her trip details with Lucy. Since her best friend was recovering from an appendectomy, Tina needed to be completely over her virus before visiting Lucy.

A couple days later, Tina put the necklace and cat earrings she'd bought for her best friend in a pretty gift bag, grabbed some snacks she'd picked up at the store the previous day, and drove to Lucy's apartment. Just thinking about sharing details of meeting the prince sent her stomach into flips.

As Tina expected, Lucy was thrilled with her gifts. When Tina described her travels—both in Italy and in Felinia—her friend's eyes widened. But when Tina gave details about her chance meeting in the airport with the prince and then later fainting and being taken inside the castle, she was afraid Lucy might pull out some stitches from her excited squeals.

"Careful, Lucy. You're healing from surgery, and you don't want to injure yourself." She giggled as Lucy clasped a hand over her gaping mouth, clearly beside herself at hearing that her best friend had not only met a handsome prince, but had been inside the castle.

Lucy sighed and looked at her friend with a dreamy gaze. "Oh, how romantic. I'm ecstatic for you, but a little envious. I mean, I'm so sorry you were sick, but you were rescued by a handsome prince." Her reaction was even more exuberant than Tina had expected, and she couldn't help laughing.

"Well, actually, it was a guard who kept me from falling and hitting my head, which I'm thankful for. But yes…Prince Reginald is not only handsome, but he's also incredibly kind." She paused, that same yearning she'd felt before engulfing her. Then she sobered. "But he's supposed to marry someone there, so he's not available. Not that I'd be in the running, especially being a peasant from Tennessee." Her last comment made them both giggle.

"Okay, that settles it." Lucy announced.

"Settles what?" Tina bit into one of the cookies she'd brought for them to share.

"We absolutely have to travel to Felinia. Who knows? Maybe you'll see Prince Charming again and I'll get to see that beautiful little island. The information and pictures I found on the internet made it look amazing. And seeing your photos and hearing details makes it seem like a paradise." The dreamy gaze returned to Lucy's eyes.

"Oh, trust me, it *is* amazing. Not just because of the handsome prince, but the island itself is beautiful. Lush and tropical, and people there seem very friendly. And the cats. There were so many cats wandering around. Of course, I loved that aspect of the island, too."

"Okay then—we must visit. We can start planning for it now." Lucy's face glowed, as though travel plans were already whirling in her mind.

"Sounds like a plan! And this will help me feel less guilty about you missing our original trip." Tina lifted a shoulder.

"Hey, it sure wasn't your fault my appendix decided to cause problems. And *you* ended up getting sick in a foreign country—although your experience sounds much better than mine. There was no royalty involved in my surgery." Lucy grinned.

Later that day, Tina kept thinking of Prince Reginald and her brief time in Felinia. Since she'd already viewed her photos countless times, she checked online to see if there was a site on Felinia that she'd previously missed when she'd searched.

To her astonishment there was a small article on Felinia's royal family that caught her eye. As she read on, her breath caught in her throat. According to the article, the prince's betrothal to a young woman named Lorie DeVenes had been called off. Was this factual or just a rumor? If other news sources also reported the information, Tina would assume it to be true.

Sure enough, when she checked two other sites

featuring articles on the small island, they posted the same update. The prince and Miss DeVenes were no longer betrothed, but none of the articles listed reasons why the couple had split, nor was there any mention of the prince's future plans.

As she pondered the article, Tina had to wonder about Miss DeVenes. She also wondered if the split was mutual, or the prince had made the decision. Surely the woman wouldn't willingly break off her betrothal to someone like Prince Reginald.

One thing was certain. The next time she and Lucy visited, they'd have more to talk about regarding Felinia's royal family.

~ ~ ~

"Wentworth, I have a note to be posted as soon as possible." Reginald braced himself for the assistant's questioning look, but he simply nodded.

"Yes, Your Highness. I will see that this is taken care of immediately."

"I'd like to request that it not end up in anyone else's hands, please."

Wentworth appeared more than a little curious as he arched a brow. "Certainly, Sire. No worries. I shall take care of this myself."

Reginald knew he didn't have to worry that the man would share anything about the note with other castle staff. The fiercely loyal assistant would do whatever necessary to further the best interest of the king and prince.

"Thank you, Wentworth." Reginald returned to his chair behind his desk. After the assistant left his office, Reginald reflected on what he'd written in the note to Tina Ransom. Not accustomed to sending mail—especially of a personal nature—to anyone in the United States, he'd been very careful of his wording and also made certain the address was written correctly. The few times he'd visited America, the country had seemed delightful, although a bit different from his small island country.

Hopefully, Miss Ransom would appreciate that he was concerned about her, given the fact she'd fainted outside of the castle. He was doing the right thing by following up on her. Yet, he had to admit another reason for sending the note. Reginald longed to be in touch with her. Was he foolish to hope that she might visit Felinia again someday?

I know nothing about her. She might have a beau or even a fiancé in her home country. The thought chided him again, as it had done while he was penning the note. Well, even if Tina had a beau, there was still no reason that Reginald couldn't check on her well-being.

Now he wondered if she'd even reply to his note. What if she didn't write back? He assumed not many people in America corresponded regularly with royalty in any country. But that didn't mean that he and Tina Ransom couldn't be long-distance friends.

Try as he might, he couldn't stop thinking about the beautiful, auburn-haired American lady with the gentle mannerisms and sweet, soft voice. In the brief time she was visiting Felinia, there were two occasions when the two of them had found themselves together. Reginald couldn't help but wonder if God had intervened and arranged their meeting. The very thought sent his pulse racing.

In the next two weeks, he didn't have much time to delve into private thoughts about Tina, because several projects demanded his attention. On a Friday morning, Wentworth tapped at his office door, reminding Reginald of a meeting in his father's office.

"Yes, thank you, Wentworth. I'll gather my notes and be on my way." He grabbed the binder containing his notes and silently told himself he must focus on business, not a certain American.

King Franklin wasn't at his desk, as he usually was for their meetings. Rather, he paced slowly, hands clasped behind his back and a slight frown on his aging face.

"Father, are you feeling well today?" Reginald glanced at Wentworth, who also appeared concerned.

"I'm fine. Just pondering the latest developments in our venture with DeVenes. It seems that he's having second thoughts and not wanting to go ahead with our joint project. At least not anytime soon. I hope the man won't start behaving like a spoiled child just because his daughter is no longer betrothed to my son." The king shook his head, the frown turning into a scowl.

A stab of guilt hit Reginald, yet he was still certain he'd done the right thing in ending the betrothal with Lorie. But for her father to end business dealings was ridiculous, and that made Reginald angry. He drew in a deep breath, carefully choosing his words.

"Father, I am terribly sorry for any problems that my decision is causing you. That's been my greatest concern all along, I'll admit. I didn't want the fact that I couldn't marry Lorie DeVenes to impact your business relationship with Mr. DeVenes." He hoped his father realized the sincerity of his words.

King Franklin stepped over to Reginald and placed a hand on his shoulder. "I know, my son. Mr. DeVenes' decision to put our business on hold is his choice, and he should be mature enough—and wise enough—to be able to continue our relationship without letting what happened with the betrothal have an impact."

He paused and shrugged. "To be quite truthful, I'm starting to wonder about the man's character if his latest business decision is due to his feelings about the ended engagement. That certainly doesn't speak highly of him, and it saddens me." He released a light *tsk* sound and shook his head. Then he looked at Reginald and Wentworth, and a smile spread across his cheeks.

"Enough of this, men. We have business to attend to, regardless of DeVenes' decisions." The king gestured for both men to have a seat as he returned to his large leather chair behind his desk.

A wave of relief washed over Reginald as he saw his father's lightened mood. The older man had had enough experiences during his reign in Felinia to know better than to allow one person's poor decision to ruin his mood. Reginald knew he still had much to learn from his father. Especially before he, himself, became the king.

For the next hour the men discussed the upcoming projects to offer assistance to the poor on their island, in addition to several other projects that required the king's input. When the meeting ended, Reginald felt a sense of accomplishment and knew that his father did too. Discussing other projects and concerns helped to take the emphasis off of Mr. DeVenes' withdrawal from working with the king, at least for the time being.

That afternoon as Reginald was catching up on some reading, Wentworth tapped at his office door. "The mail has arrived, Your Highness." The assistant's voice held a note of amusement. He stepped over to Reginald and handed him an envelope with lovely handwriting, postmarked from the United States. After a slight hesitation, Wentworth nodded and exited the room.

Reginald's pulse raced. A letter from America! He didn't want to rip it open, so he used his sterling silver letter opener. Before sliding the sharp piece under the envelope's flap, he looked closely at the top left corner of the envelope. Good. Her name and address were clearly written—Tina Ransom from Tennessee.

His hands were shaking. *Calm down. She most likely appreciated my help when she fainted, nothing more.* Yet, the fact that he had indeed received a reply from Tina gave his heart a lift.

Blowing out a long sigh, Reginald carefully opened the envelope and lifted out the lovely notecard with colorful flowers on the front. Very feminine. He began to read, and then re-read, his heart beating faster with each word.

As he'd predicted, this was a thank-you note for his note to her, for the brief tour of the artifacts room at the airport, and for his staff providing care after she'd fainted in front of the castle.

She went on to write that she'd been very embarrassed, but at the time was sicker than she'd realized from a virus she'd had. The remainder of her note expressed how impressed she'd been with the beauty of Felinia, not to mention the friendliness and hospitality of the island people.

But her closing lines caused Reginald's heart to race with joy, and he re-read them several times to make sure he was interpreting her message accurately. She stated that she was planning to return to the island in the near future, along with her friend named Lucy. A small smiling face accompanied her signature, much like one a young child might draw. It made Reginald grin, and also reminded him that Tina worked with young children.

His spirits soared. He had told himself that perhaps Tina would respond to the note he'd sent, but he assumed it would be a polite reply. He'd never dreamed she would mention returning to Felinia. Now he needed to pray that her trip would come to pass, if it was the Lord's will.

The next morning Reginald decided to pen a response to Tina's note. He didn't want to come across as being forward, but he was eager to let her know he was happy that she planned on returning. He also asked if she would please notify him of her arrival dates ahead of time, adding that if his schedule allowed, he'd make certain Tina and her friend received a thorough tour of Felinia's most scenic spots.

But his heart told him there was no question about his schedule, because once he learned she was headed back to his island, he'd make certain his days were free to spend time with the lovely lady from America.

~ ~ ~

"I hope my note to Prince Reginald was appropriate. After all, I know nothing about royal etiquette." Tina blew out a sigh as she adjusted the thermostat in her small apartment. The July heat was taking a toll on her energy level.

Lucy sat on the living room sofa, fanning herself with a magazine. "Thanks, girlfriend. It was getting a bit toasty in here." She grinned. "And don't worry about the note you wrote to Prince Charming. It sounded perfect to me." Lucy giggled, then lifted her glass of iced tea off the table. The two friends had been enjoying a leisurely visit that day, wanting to make the most of their free time before school began.

"Okay, thanks for reassuring me. Now we need to look at our calendars and see when we can work out this little trip. I'm glad we're both teachers so we have the same vacation days off." Tina opened her planner. "Can't believe July is zipping along. It seems like the 4th of July arrived sooner this year. I'm just glad you felt like attending the town parade with me." She grinned, remembering how Lucy had teased her about not fainting in the heat that day.

"Too bad we can't go while it's still summer. But since school starts back so early now, we'll have to wait." Lucy shrugged.

"How about our fall break in late September? Now that our school system is using a revised calendar for the school year, we'll have a week-long break then." Tina hoped the timing would work out so the prince could meet them—even briefly. Her pulse raced just thinking about it.

"Yes, that should work. I don't have anything planned for that week. The next break after that is Thanksgiving, so we wouldn't want to be away during a holiday time." Lucy eyed her cell phone calendar and nodded thoughtfully.

After discussing their possible travel plans and

how they each planned to use their remaining summer break time, Lucy returned home. As Tina peered once again at her calendar, it struck her that she and her best friend were actually planning to visit the tropical island and might even visit with the prince. Now she was eager for the new school year to begin. The sooner school started, the sooner their fall break would arrive.

She only hoped that this time, neither she nor Lucy became sick. Tina was also thankful her current financial situation allowed her to take another trip. With a tug at her heart, she couldn't help thinking that her parents would be happy for her, if they were still alive. And she was certain her brother would be all for her planned trip with Lucy, since he'd encouraged their original trip before Lucy became sick.

That evening, Tina's cell phone rang, and she answered without checking the caller ID. Big mistake. Her ex-boyfriend's voice came through, and Tina's stomach clenched. Why was Chuck calling her now? Their relationship had ended months ago, and not too soon for her.

Tina wouldn't be rude, but she had no interest at all in having a conversation with him. He'd shown his true colors and she had learned a lesson about trusting her gut instinct when something felt off. She should've known he was seeing other women while they dated. Apparently, he'd been on a major ego-trip and thought by having several relationships at once, he was more of a man. Ha. The opposite was true in Tina's eyes.

After listening to him ramble on about his new motorcycle and getting a raise at work, Tina was about to tell him she needed to go. Before she could, he asked her for a date. It was all she could do not to click off her phone right then, but she managed to remain polite and tell him no, that wouldn't be a good idea.

As expected, he began his old apology spiel, saying he'd made a big mistake not treating her better. *Too bad. You had your chance, and I learned a lesson.* Tina didn't verbalize her thoughts, but again stated that she could not go out with him. "Take care." After the brief statement, she didn't give him a chance to say more but clicked off her phone.

Tomorrow, she'd tell Lucy about the unexpected phone call, but for tonight, she'd only allow happy thoughts to fill her mind. Such as planning a fun visit to a small island inhabited by a handsome prince.

The irony struck her just then—what a world of difference between the prince and her ex-boyfriend. Even if Reginald hadn't been part of a royal family, he didn't seem the type to deceive a woman he cared about, although Tina knew little about him.

She couldn't help wonder, though, what had led to the prince's betrothal being called off. It would likely come out in some reports, but Tina would be careful what she believed. Those tabloids often didn't report the truth, and she didn't want garbage to tarnish her impression of the prince. Still, she was curious and hoped the Prince of Felinia was as upstanding as he seemed.

~ ~ ~

Reginald was still concerned about Lorie's father backing out of the business dealings with King Franklin. There was the chance Mr. DeVenes would change his mind, but the more Reginald thought it over, the more anger built up inside him. He finally opened up to Wentworth.

"I hate to admit this is troubling me so much, but the way Mr. DeVenes is behaving is ridiculous. Regardless of any relationship—or lack thereof—between the man's daughter and myself, it should have absolutely no bearing at all on business between him and my father. It angers me." Reginald clenched his fists, then released them. Maybe he needed to get more physical exercise and fresh air so the man didn't get to him.

Wentworth nodded, his face revealing he agreed completely. "Sire, I could not have worded it better myself. I've often thought that someone should perhaps remind Mr. DeVenes he is an adult, not a child." Wentworth shook his head.

A moment later, the assistant's face brightened. "I have to say, Your Highness, that it's good your father's business matters are not completely dependent on Mr. DeVenes. As you well know, King Franklin has other profitable ventures that have nothing to do with DeVenes. If the man chooses to continue being childish over business matters due to a broken betrothal, then we shall say it is his loss." Wentworth gestured with his hands, as if wiping them clean.

Reginald fought hard to stifle a laugh that wanted to escape. Seeing the stoic assistant become so animated was enjoyable to watch. Yet he knew that Wentworth was again displaying his unwavering loyalty to the royal family of Felinia, and he appreciated it.

"Thank you, Wentworth. That's an excellent way of viewing the entire matter. I've been wondering if he actually thought withholding business dealings with

Father would perhaps cause me to change my mind about wanting to marry his daughter."

Reginald knew in his heart that a marriage to Lorie DeVenes would indeed be a grave mistake. No doubt he'd end up miserable, and she might also. Or she would end up making him even more miserable. No, that was no way for a marriage to start, royal or otherwise.

Feeling better after his encouragement from Wentworth, Reginald focused on his current projects for the next few days, including doing more for the residents on the west side of the island. Sadly, there were still reports of people living in poverty in that section, and Reginald wanted to eradicate poverty on the island altogether. Some may call that an impossible feat, but he would do his best.

On Friday afternoon, Wentworth tapped at his office door. "A letter for you, Your Highness." He held out the small envelope, his eyes sparkling, then he turned and exited the room.

As soon as the door closed, Reginald carefully opened the envelope, not wanting to tear even a tiny piece of it. The same delicate, feminine handwriting let him know even before he saw the return name and address that this was from Tina. Just as he'd done with her first note, Reginald read with shaking hands, then re-read three times. She was planning another visit to Felinia! He could scarcely believe it.

Hurrying to look at his calendar for the month of September, he was relieved there was nothing major on the schedule. He was especially thankful there were no trips, even though he and his father didn't travel much. However, there was an occasional flight to another country for a goodwill visit.

He sat for a few minutes absorbing this wonderful news. Then it hit him that he would have to handle this situation with the utmost care. Without a doubt Wentworth could be trusted, yet he would have to take extra care that no other castle staff members got word of Tina visiting Felinia. Especially since word about the 'American lady who'd fainted in front of the castle' had made the front page for a few days.

First and foremost, he'd need to speak with his father and let him know about Tina and her friend visiting in September. Would it be permissible to welcome them for a meal at the castle? Surely if his father was present it wouldn't cause a scandal. He hated having to be so cautious about such a matter, yet that was part of living life as a member of a royal family. There were positive and negative aspects, and being in the public eye would rank as a negative, at least in Reginald's opinion.

Abruptly, he felt a niggle of guilt. Reginald needed to pray and thank the Lord for allowing this to happen. He bowed his head and gave thanks, asking for safe travels for Tina and her friend. He added a plea that if a real relationship was possible, for the Lord to show him the way.

After the brief but heartfelt prayer, Reginald felt better. The past couple of weeks had taken a toll on his emotions. Breaking the betrothal with Lorie DeVenes, and then her father's decision to withdraw from business dealings with his father, had drained him more than he'd realized. But receiving another note from Tina saying that she was returning to Felinia in two months gave him a bright ray of hope. His spirits lifted more than they had in a long time.

Reginald stepped to his favorite window, looking out at the courtyard with its emerald green shrubs, all perfectly manicured with colorful blooms placed in between, creating a feast for the eyes. A summer breeze blew in from the sea, and birds chirped in the tree branches, as if aware of the prince's excitement and wanting to join in the happy day.

Yes, it truly was a happy day, and he could hardly wait to tell his father. But he needed to continue praying that all would go smoothly, because sometimes events happened out of his control. But for now, he relished the joy he felt after reading her note and would allow himself to indulge in thoughts of a beautiful American tourist named Tina Ransom.

~ ~ ~

"Shall I summon a doctor, Your Majesty?" Wentworth's words to the king caused Reginald's pulse to race as he entered his father's office later that day. What was going on?

King Franklin released a raspy cough and shook his head, then held a hand up, indicating he needed to catch his breath. Why did he sound so wheezy?

Reginald hurried over to where his father sat by a window, and noticed right away that he was pale and clutched a linen handkerchief. He leaned in closer and lowered his voice, "Father, what's wrong?"

The king looked up and shook his head. "No, just a nagging cough that has taken up residence in my chest. I just need some cough syrup, although I don't like taking medicine of any kind." He shook his head, then released another cough.

Reginald and Wentworth exchanged a look of concern. "Wentworth, would you please see that my father gets the cough medicine he needs? If he continues with this cough, we'll have to summon Dr. Foster."

"Yes, Sire. I agree completely." The assistant turned to the king. "With all due respect, Your Majesty, we do not want this cough to develop into something much worse."

The king peered up at his assistant with a resigned look. He held out his arthritic hands palms up, as if gesturing to them he was too tired to argue.

"I shall get the medicine and find a maid to bring hot tea. Perhaps that will be soothing for his cough." Wentworth turned and strode out the king's office door. Out in the hall, he summoned Genevieve to bring tea for King Franklin.

Reginald didn't want to leave his father's side. News about Tina's planned trip in September could wait another day.

Another coughing spell overtook the king. It was obvious he didn't feel well.

"Father, you need some bedrest." He braced himself for the king's rebuttal.

To Reginald's great surprise and even greater concern, his father offered no resistance.

Seated in a chair near his father's side, Reginald pointed out some of the lovely blooms in the courtyard and commented on the summer weather. Soon Wentworth returned with the cough medicine and Genevieve scurried in carrying a silver tray with a small teapot, cups, and a plate of cookies.

She bowed slightly, concern etched on her face.

"Here you are, Your Majesty. I do hope this tea will help calm your cough. I'm so sorry you're not feeling well."

The king looked up at the maid with tired eyes. "Thank you, Genevieve. And I'd prefer if word didn't spread that I am ill. I know that often well-meaning people can exaggerate the facts, and I don't want the island thinking I'm headed to a hospital." A weak grin appeared as he looked at the maid again.

Genevieve blushed and smiled, lowering her eyes. "Certainly, Your Majesty. No one else needs to know you're not feeling well. Please, if there is anything else I can bring for you, I will be more than happy to do so." She bowed again, this time more pronounced since she was no longer clutching the silver tea tray.

The king thanked her again before his cough took hold.

Wentworth stayed nearby, as did Reginald, encouraging him to sip the tea after taking a dose of the cough medicine. Although the king took his medicine with a grimace, and then sipped his hot tea, he declined the offer of a cookie.

As soon as his father was feeling better, he'd tell him about Tina and make sure of the protocol for a female visitor. Even though he was concerned about his father's health, for the remainder of that day, his thoughts were lifted each time he re-read the note from America.

~ ~ ~

Chapter 7

The remainder of July seemed to fly by for Tina, and before she knew it, early August had arrived and the week for teachers to prepare for the upcoming school year. When she and Lucy took a lunch break together on Wednesday of that week, they both bemoaned the fact that pre-planning seemed to start earlier each year.

Then Lucy brightened as she shared a thought. "Just think, Tina. The sooner we start this school year, the sooner our September break will roll around. And you know what that means." She waggled her eyebrows.

Tina giggled, knowing exactly what her bestie meant. "Yep, our adventure to Felinia. I still can't believe we have plans to go in late September. I'll admit that I've made myself not think about it too much and try to focus on plans for my new kindergarten students. But when I do think about it, I practically squeal. Mainly because I can't wait for you to see that gorgeous   little island, Lucy. My photos don't do it justice." She sighed and finished her salad.

Lucy smiled. "Well, your photos were very impressive, so I'm counting down the days until we go. And even if we don't get a glimpse of your Prince Charming, it'll be okay. Just seeing that gorgeous, tropical paradise will be heavenly." A dreamy sigh followed her words.

As it turned out, Tina barely had time to think about anything other than her teaching job in the next few weeks. She always seemed to forget how hectic each new school year was. How could her co-workers who had children of their own manage the start of a new school year and a family?

But she loved her job and couldn't imagine doing anything else. Her two dozen new students captured her heart—and her energy—and kept her mind from dwelling on Felinia or a certain prince. Yet, each time she read a fairy tale to her students, Tina felt a thrill when the story featured a prince or king. In fact, one day in mid-September, one of her young students asked why she smiled each time she mentioned the story's prince. *Busted.*

When Tina shared the incident with Lucy over lunch that next Saturday, Lucy spewed out a laugh. "How did you respond to that observant kiddo?"

"I just told her that I enjoy reading about royal families." Tina giggled.

Unfortunately, Tina didn't like the article she read online a few days later. As was her custom these days, she'd look for information about Felinia about twice a week—just to see if anything had been posted, news-related or weather-related. The article that grabbed her attention caused her heart to pound. Uh-oh. She didn't want to read it, but she did.

The article stated that a spokesman for the DeVenes family of Italy recently held a briefing stating that Lorie DeVenes's betrothal had ended due to infidelity on the part of the prince. Although there were no specifics, the implications were clear. Miss DeVenes had stated that she was glad the truth came to light before she entered into a marriage with Prince Reginald.

Tina's hands shook as she scrolled through listings to find more articles with this same information. Thankfully, she didn't find anything else, but still…was the article she'd read actually true? If not, what a horrible thing to say about the prince. Tina grabbed her cell phone and immediately called Lucy to share what she'd found.

"Wow, I'll have to take a look, but do you think this is a reputable source, or is it one of those trash-talking tabloids?" Lucy was right. It could just be yellow journalism.

"I have no idea. But I hope and pray this isn't true, Lucy. We can still visit Felinia like we'd planned, but how disappointing if the prince isn't as wonderful as he seemed. Even the hotel staff spoke highly of him, and a nice man I met on the shuttle there had mentioned there was never any scuttlebutt about the prince or the king." Tina released a long sigh.

"Okay, we'll see if anything else comes out about this. But try not to be too upset. Think of all the stories that are printed here in the States that are just flat-out false. I'm sure it's the same way everywhere, unfortunately."

When the call ended, Tina tried to shove the

article out of her mind and focus on ideas for her young students. And when the fall break arrived, the two best friends would still take a trip and have fun, regardless of any royal rumors.

~ ~ ~

"This is preposterous." Reginald's pulse raced and his head began to throb. He and Wentworth had met to discuss the best way of handling the absurd, false article that appeared in a small tabloid.

"Your Highness, this is absolute trash, and I'd venture to say that the people of Felinia realize this is not true. Still, we must issue a statement, of course." Wentworth's normally stoic countenance now showed evidence of dismay, his face reddened, and his eyebrows furrowed.

As angry as Reginald was by this printed lie, he was mostly concerned about the effect it might have on his father's health. Especially since the king was already fighting a bad cough. When he expressed his concern to the assistant, Wentworth held up his palm.

"Your Highness, we will write a statement and I'll give it to Collins. He will ensure the statement is published and not to be questioned. We will also inform the staff that this ridiculous lie is not to be mentioned to King Franklin under any circumstances. When you deem the time is right, then you can mention this to your father, if you wish."

Reginald nodded and thanked Wentworth, knowing that Alfred Collins, a distant cousin of King Franklin and the castle's public-relations man, would handle this situation.

Why had Lorie DeVenes done this? Especially

after appearing to handle their break-up in a somewhat calm manner. Reginald replayed that day in his mind, remembering how she'd not seemed too surprised and had only shed minimal tears. It wasn't as though the woman had been heartbroken and sobbing. *Or that there'd ever been a hint of love in their relationship.*

Wentworth cleared his throat, and it was almost as though he'd read the prince's mind. "You know, Sire, there's an old saying about a woman scorned. This is likely what this lie is all about. It's highly possible that Miss DeVenes is embarrassed that her royal wedding isn't going to happen, after all. Rather than allow speculation to sully her reputation, it was easier to paint you in a negative light. Sadly, I've read about this happening in other situations." Wentworth shook his head.

Reginald began to pace. "You're most likely correct. As much as I hate to say this, I always had the feeling that Lorie was more in love with the idea of marrying into royalty than she was with me." He stopped short of adding that in truth, he didn't think Lorie had loved him at all, and it was mutual. Yes, he'd definitely done the right thing in ending the betrothal, even if he must deal with the aftermath now.

For the next half-hour, the two men discussed the appropriate response to the scandal, and then Wentworth left the prince's office to type the notice and deliver it to Collins. Reginald felt drained, just as he'd been after their meeting with the DeVenes family to call off the betrothal. Perhaps the king was better off not having Mr. DeVenes as a business partner in any type of venture. He might not be as trustworthy as the king had originally thought.

Before heading to check on his father, Reginald lifted up a silent prayer for wisdom. He'd not had much experience dealing with negative situations such as this one, and he wanted to handle it in the best way. What a blessing Wentworth was.

After praying, Reginald stepped to his door to exit his office and visit the king. A sudden thought made him halt his steps. What if the article had reached the United States and Tina read it? With technology, anything was possible where printed stories—true or not—were concerned. The thought made his gut clench.

Should he write to Tina and tell her that he was aware of a negative, false story that had been written? Or should he treat the situation as though it had never happened? But another question formed in his mind that bothered him even more. What if Tina cancelled her planned trip to Felinia? That would be devastating. Because even though he didn't want to admit it, Reginald had been looking forward to seeing the beautiful American again. A lot.

~ ~ ~

Tina kept reminding herself that she and Lucy were planning a trip to Felinia to see the beautiful island, not to visit a member of the royal family on said island. But as their travel date drew closer, she became more anxious.

It didn't help when Tina received a call from Lucy, who'd discovered another article online about the Prince of Felinia being unfaithful to his betrothed, Lorie DeVenes of Italy. Lucy tried to reassure Tina it was likely untrue. "You know how those tabloids are. Nobody actually believes what they read in those publications. I only wanted you to be aware that more trash had been written about the prince."

Tina appreciated her best friend's efforts, and she kept hoping that it truly was 'trash,' as Lucy had called the article. Maybe the women should've planned another trip to Italy, rather than Felinia. Yet each time she viewed her photos, or simply thought about Felinia, her heart tugged with that yearning to see the tiny island again. There was something almost enchanting about the place—even if she'd not met the prince in person.

On the Tuesday after Labor Day, Tina received another letter from the prince. After opening it with trembling hands, she began to read, her heart racing with each line.

Prince Reginald had written that he still hoped she and her friend were planning to visit, and if possible, he'd like to see Tina again and meet her friend. He'd also written that regretfully, some false rumors had plagued him, and if those rumors had reached news outlets in the States, he sincerely hoped Tina would ignore them. He even added that he couldn't say more in the note, but looked forward to their visit, if Tina's schedule allowed.

Her heart soared. She immediately phoned Lucy to read the note to her.

"See? I told you it was trash. The poor prince. That DeVenes woman must be a character if she's the one who started the rumors." Lucy was talking rapidly, a sure sign she was excited about this update. Tina couldn't help smiling as she listened to her friend.

"You're right. And he looks forward to visiting with us, Lucy."

"I know! A real prince is hoping you can squeeze

him into your travel plans," Lucy giggled.

After the call ended, Tina's spirits soared. She'd been praying that if she and Lucy were not supposed to travel to Felinia, that the Lord would give her a clear sign. But with the prince's encouraging note, wasn't that a sign that the friends *should* go? Tina finally allowed herself to be excited about the trip, rather than second-guessing her decision. Besides, her brother had also encouraged the trip with Lucy, especially since her bestie had missed the original trip during the summer.

Her eyes landed on a framed photo of her parents, and her eyes pooled with moisture. How she missed them, but Tina genuinely felt her parents would encourage her to travel if they'd still been alive.

A sudden thought ushered a smile. While she'd been busy planning the trip to Felinia with Lucy, Tina hadn't once thought about her fear of flying. After her parents' untimely death, Tina had wondered if she'd ever again be able to fly, yet she'd managed the flight to Italy on her own, even with turbulence and an unscheduled stop on the small island.

Tina would've never imagined how the events of the past summer had impacted her life. Not only helping her to overcome the fear of flying again, but also discovering a paradise she'd never known existed, all due to her plane having engine trouble.

She'd always heard that the Lord worked in mysterious ways, and that He could use negative situations for good. That had certainly been true in her life, she realized now, although Lucy had missed their original trip, and then Tina had become sick in Felinia. Yet if those things had not happened, she likely wouldn't be planning the trip to Felinia now.

Her biggest challenge in the upcoming days was keeping her mind focused on her job, rather than her upcoming trip. But Tina didn't need to worry about that, because her kindergarten students kept her fully occupied while she was at school. Just another reminder of why she loved her job so much.

~ ~ ~

"Here we go!" Tina smiled at Lucy, seated beside her on the plane as it taxied along the runway. After lifting countless prayers for safe travels, Tina was determined to relax as much as possible and enjoy this trip with her best friend.

The friends had flown from Knoxville to Atlanta and were now seated on their connecting flight from Atlanta to the island of Felinia. Tina knew that Lucy would keep her entertained on the long flight, and she was right. The time seemed to pass quickly as the women chatted about their students and plans for the remainder of the school year. Then Tina scrolled through her photos of Felinia on her phone, answering Lucy's questions about different pictures.

Tina didn't miss the grin on Lucy's face when Tina mentioned the prince. She wanted to be careful not to let her best friend know just how attractive she found him, although she had shared the yearning she'd felt toward the small island. Tina chalked it up to an infatuation. After all, who wouldn't be drawn to a tropical island inhabited by a handsome prince?

Thankfully, the flight went smoothly and landed without a problem on the small, island runway of Felinia. The friends were relieved to see the hotel shuttle parked at the curb, ready to take travelers to the

Felinia hotel. Tina almost pinched herself to make certain she wasn't dreaming, but Lucy's constant excited chatter reminded her that she was, indeed, wide awake.

"I love this island already." Lucy commented after the brief drive from the airport to the hotel. "And I've only seen a little bit of it…but it's gorgeous." Lucy's eyes held that dreamy look she'd had when hearing Tina describe the island.

"Just wait. You'll fall in love with Felinia as quickly as I did."

"Hey, does the prince have a brother?" Lucy playfully teased. "Then we could each have a royal boyfriend."

Tina lightly shoulder-bumped her friend. "Don't forget that you already have a boyfriend in Tennessee. A boyfriend who adores you."

"Yes, I know, and I adore him, too. I think I'm just caught up in the spell of this beautiful place." She winked at Tina.

As the group of tourists entered the lobby of the Felinia hotel, the friendly desk clerk greeted the group right away. When the man spotted Tina, he beamed. "Ah, Miss Tina. So happy you're visiting us again."

Tina was touched that Giovanni recognized her and remembered her name, even though she knew her face must be beet-red. She returned his smile and offered a quick greeting, not missing the curious stares of the other tourists.

Lucy whispered, clearly impressed, "Wow. You've made quite an impression here."

Tina shrugged and reminded Lucy that the kind man had been very helpful on her previous visit.

After settling in their hotel room, the friends decided to walk to a nearby café. They agreed that after the long flight and the time difference, they'd wait until the next morning to sightsee.

Tina was especially eager to ride the island shuttle service to the castle, but she refused to get her hopes up about seeing the prince again. If things worked out that they were able to see him, that would be wonderful. But she didn't want to anticipate that and be disappointed. Nor did she want Lucy to be disappointed, either.

The next morning, the women headed again to the nearby café for breakfast, then began their day of sightseeing. Since they'd only be in Felinia for a few days, they wanted to make the most of their time.

Thoughts of the prince hovered at the back of Tina's mind, wherever they walked. She suggested to Lucy that the following day they could take an island shuttle to see more of the island—specifically the area where the castle was located.

"You're my personal tour guide," Lucy teased her. "Since this is actually your third visit to the island." She giggled.

Tina rolled her eyes. "Yeah, if you're counting the emergency landing my plane had on the way to Italy. But that time I only toured the airport." *And I met the prince.* She didn't add that thought aloud, knowing she'd blush.

After browsing delightful gift shops, trying a different café for an early supper, and accruing lots of steps, the women returned to their hotel. As they passed by the counter, Giovanni called out to Tina.

"You have a message, Miss Tina." His dark eyes held amusement as he extended a small cream-colored envelope toward her.

"Thank you, Giovanni." She then turned to Lucy.

"I hope nothing is wrong back home." Tina clutched the envelope as the women stepped onto the elevator. "I'll read it when we're inside our room."

Once she'd thrown her backpack on her bed, Tina examined the envelope as Lucy gasped, "What's that on the back?"

Tina carefully turned it over to see an official-looking seal on the envelope's flap—a *royal* seal. Her heart raced as realization dawned on her. No, this wasn't a message about anyone in Tennessee, this note was from the castle. Now she understood the sparkle in Giovanni's eyes.

Lucy leaned in for a closer look, clearly as excited as Tina about this unexpected note. "Hurry and read it, but be careful that you don't tear that fancy seal. I have a feeling you'll want to save that for your scrapbook." She giggled.

With shaking hands, Tina gently unsealed the small envelope, and lifted out a folded note. She read the note aloud to Lucy.

"You and your friend are invited for tea at the castle tomorrow at two o'clock. A shuttle will arrive for you at the hotel, if you're able to attend. No reply is needed. In the event you cannot attend, please notify the head desk clerk at your hotel, and he will relay the message to our courier. Sincerely, Prince Reginald of Felinia"

For a few moments, neither woman spoke, but stared at each other with widened eyes. Then with giddy voices, they both babbled at once about being invited to tea with a real prince.

For the remainder of that evening, the friends discussed what to wear the next day and wondered what the experience would hold. Not surprisingly, Tina had trouble falling asleep that night, and only hoped she wouldn't be so tired the next day that she collapsed at the castle. After all, she'd done that once already. She couldn't let that happen again.

~ ~ ~

Prince Reginald awakened the next morning with a sense of anticipation, but also a bit of nervousness. How silly, he told himself. Hosting two American ladies for tea at the castle was hardly a reason to feel nervous. But he wanted everything to go smoothly and his guests to have a pleasant time. To his relief, he'd not received a message from the hotel indicating the ladies couldn't attend.

And, lest he deceive himself, he especially wanted time to learn more about the auburn-haired beauty from the United States. He only hoped she didn't mention being engaged. But if so, he'd have to act happy for her.

Wentworth had gone along with his plans, although Reginald could tell that his assistant wasn't overly fond of the idea. Reginald had emphasized that this was simply an informal, friendly social event, to show hospitality to two American tourists. There was no way he'd even hint at the fact he found Miss Ransom quite appealing.

Even though the older man had never voiced his thoughts on the topic, Reginald suspected Wentworth thought it best for the prince to marry into a family with royal ties or at least with a lengthy pedigree. Did Wentworth deem it a waste of time to entertain someone who wasn't of royal lineage or well-known in certain elite social circles?

But where had that gotten him previously? In a miserable betrothal that ended up being broken. The more he thought about that situation, the more relieved Reginald was that he was no longer engaged to Lorie DeVenes. He almost felt queasy at the thought of what might've happened and how miserable he would've been.

After breakfast, Reginald checked on his father. Although King Franklin was still coughing and somewhat weak, he was responding to the strong medications, so that was encouraging. Reginald couldn't help noticing that his father's spirits seemed lighter too and felt certain it was due in part to relief. Ending the betrothal had been a burden on the king, too, but now it was behind them.

Reginald had decided not to mention his upcoming tea with the American ladies until closer to the event. After leaving his father's room, Reginald headed to his office and met with Wentworth.

"So, everything is set for my tea this afternoon? No problems?"

Wentworth smiled, although it appeared a bit strained. "Yes, Your Highness. Everything is set, and there are no problems. I have given the kitchen staff strict instructions that this visit is to remain confidential for security purposes, and they've all sworn they will cooperate."

"Very good. Thank you, Wentworth." He nodded at the assistant, who now appeared more relaxed. "Since protocol dictates that you will need to be close by, you are certainly welcome to join us for tea. You might enjoy visiting with these ladies from America."

Wentworth's eyes opened wide, but he shook his head as his face turned crimson. "Thank you, Sire, but I should decline your offer. At least for this time. This will be your special visit with your American guests, so you don't need a middle-aged man hovering and trying to join the conversation." The corners of his mouth turned up slightly.

Then he quickly added, "However, Your Highness, I sincerely appreciate your invitation. I will remain close by and will assist with anything if needed, but the visit itself is for you and your special guests."

Had he imagined that his assistant had seemed to emphasize the word *special* as though indicating that two young ladies visiting from America was a significant event indeed?

After feeling confident that everything was in order, Reginald was ready to focus on the rest of his morning and make it a productive one. He and Wentworth discussed several projects and upcoming meetings, then the assistant exited the office while Reginald jotted some notes in his planner. Yet, he couldn't concentrate, because his mind kept returning to Tina and her friend.

Imagining how they must feel being invited to a castle by a prince almost made him chuckle. Of course, he had no idea how Tina and her friend would feel, but he was certain this would be an exciting event for them. All the more reason for everything to go smoothly. And, of course, there was no reason for things not to go smoothly, especially with Wentworth overseeing the event. Thankfully, their recent good weather had continued, with no rain predicted.

Now his only concern was making sure he didn't act like a foolish youth when his visitors were at the castle. Because as often as he'd thought about Tina since meeting her, Reginald was afraid he might behave more like a lovestruck adolescent rather than a prince. Hopefully, with his assistant nearby, he would maintain the level of decorum he needed to display to his guests.

But he had to admit that he would like nothing more than to have a small amount of time alone with Tina, just to gaze into her green eyes and hear her sweet, gentle voice. Was it possible that might happen someday? He'd keep praying, because he wasn't getting any younger.

~ ~ ~

Promptly at two o'clock, Tina and Lucy boarded the shuttle outside their hotel. The kind hotel clerk had inclined his head in a knowing way and told them to enjoy their day, his eyes twinkling as though he knew where they were headed.

Sitting on the shuttle with no other passengers, the women kept their voices lowered so the driver wouldn't overhear, not that he was paying any attention. Lucy squeezed Tina's arm and whispered, "What if I faint? I'm so excited, but nervous too."

Tina released a shaky giggle. "If you faint, I can testify from experience that a nice castle guard will assist you." Both women laughed, trying not to distract the driver.

When they arrived, they stepped off the shuttle where a guard greeted them.

"If you'll follow me, please." The guard spoke in clipped English while maintaining a serious demeanor.

The two friends followed him along a cobblestone walkway, and Tina couldn't help grinning when she saw Lucy's reaction to seeing the castle.

"It's beautiful! Look at those windows and the turrets." It was obvious Lucy was trying not to gawk but the surroundings captivated her, just as they had Tina on her previous time there—and again today.

"So gorgeous." Lucy whispered the words as the women marveled at a small fountain with water bubbling out, colorful flower beds lining the courtyard, and lush, green grass that resembled carpet. Birds twittered in the branches of the few trees spaced throughout the yard.

The guard paused by a high wooden gate and nodded. "This way, please. His Highness will join you in the east courtyard." He held the gate for the women to pass through. A side door of the castle opened, and two men came out into the courtyard.

Tina saw that one was Prince Reginald and the other was the man who'd been with him at the airport when she'd met him. Her heart pounded and her palms sweated. She needed to calm down, so she sent up a quick silent prayer and slowed her breathing.

The guard disappeared through the wooden gate, presumably returning to his station of duty in front of the castle. Tina and Lucy froze as they stood and stared at the two men approaching them.

Prince Reginald extended his right hand to Tina, then to Lucy. "Welcome, ladies. I'm so glad you could join me for tea. This is my assistant, Wentworth." The assistant nodded politely and offered a slight smile, but for the most part remained quite serious.

The prince's eyes lingered on Tina and he

grinned. "How have you been, Miss Ransom?"

It was a wonder she didn't collapse right then and there, but that would've ruined everything. She wanted this to be special not just for herself, but also for her best friend.

"I've been well, Prince Reginald. And you?"

"Very well, thank you. I am assuming this lovely lady is your friend you've mentioned?" He turned his attention to Lucy.

Before Tina could make introductions, her friend's voice came out in a squeaky tone. "Yes, I'm Lucy Young. I am honored to meet you, Prince Reginald." Lucy's face was beet-red, and Tina only hoped she wouldn't attempt a curtsy. As nervous as poor Lucy was, she'd likely fall onto the cobblestones.

Wentworth led the little group to an area of chairs underneath a large shade tree. Birds chirped in the branches above them and butterflies fluttered around the bushes of colorful blooms. Although the afternoon temperature was warm, it wasn't unpleasant, due to a light breeze blowing and the shade tree shielding them from direct sunlight. Windchimes made from seaglass hung from tree branches, sending tinkling notes on the breeze.

After the women had taken their seats, the prince lowered his tall physique into a chair facing them. There was a small round table in the middle of the group, covered with a pastel blue cloth and a small vase of red roses in the center.

"One of our maids will serve tea and cookies soon, but we'll visit a bit first. How do you both like Felinia?" The prince sat back in his chair, looking handsome and regal yet comfortable and relaxed. How did he do that?

Tina and Lucy took turns assuring him that they both were captivated by his beautiful, island country. He also questioned them about their teaching jobs in America and some of the differences they'd noticed between their hometown and Felinia. To Tina's relief, the visit was going well and Lucy's shoulders relaxed.

Minutes later, a woman who appeared to be in her forties stepped out of the castle, grasping a large silver tray with a teapot, a sugar bowl and cream pitcher, linen napkins, and a china plate of delicate tea cookies. She smiled at the women as she set the tray on the small table.

Another younger maid had followed her carrying a tray containing three cups and saucers, which appeared to be of fine china. The younger woman also smiled at Tina and Lucy, but didn't appear as self-assured as the first maid.

The prince stood and gestured to the women, which was a kind thing to do. "Ladies, this is Genevieve and this is Hilda." He turned toward the two uniformed women before looking at his guests. "And these are my special visitors from America, Miss Tina Ransom and her friend, Miss Lucy Young." The maids bowed toward the guests.

"Is there anything else we may bring you and your guests, Your Highness?" Genevieve asked, her eyes holding a spark of curiosity.

"No, thank you, Genevieve. This looks delightful. Thank you and Hilda for your assistance."

Again, the maids bowed slightly and then turned to head back inside the castle.

Tina must be dreaming. How could this be real?

Yet it was, because a cool breeze caressed her face, and her best friend sat only two feet away from her. But the fact that a handsome prince also sat nearby made this scene similar to one of the story books she read to her students.

The experience was even better than Tina could have imagined. The prince appeared genuinely interested in their lives in the United States, and he spoke about his few visits to the states. He also seemed fascinated that both ladies were teachers, and added a comment that caused both Tina and Lucy to blush. "Our small country could use more excellent teachers, if you should ever decide to re-locate." Dimples appeared on his cheeks, and Tina had to set her teacup down for fear she'd spill it onto her lap.

About twenty minutes later, Wentworth appeared and waited for an ebb in the conversation. "Your Highness, are you ready for the ladies to visit inside the castle?"

Tina and Lucy shot wide-eyed glances at each other. Tina thought her heart might burst out of her chest. When she'd fainted on her previous trip, the guard had taken her inside the castle, but in her weakened state at the time, she wasn't able to appreciate her surroundings.

Wentworth led the way and the prince strolled behind them as they entered a large side door into the stone building. With wide eyes, Lucy released a small gasp and squeezed Tina's hand. Her friend was about to burst with excitement, and she was thankful Lucy didn't actually release her usual squeal.

They stood in an entrance hallway that was lovely, even though it wasn't an actual room. The carpet on the floor felt like cushions beneath their feet. Small table lamps placed here and there in the hallway added a cozy welcoming glow to the area. They followed Wentworth into the same large parlor where Tina had been taken when she'd been ill, but this time she could enjoy it much more.

The assistant gestured toward the elegant velvet sofa along one wall, and before lowering her body onto the softness, Tina admired a large painting that hung behind the sofa. "How lovely." She gestured toward the painting and turned to the prince.

"Thank you. My uncle painted that of one of Felinia's beach areas. I've always thought it was lovely too. He had an amazing talent with a paintbrush. Sadly, he's no longer with us, but I'm thankful we can display many of his paintings here in the castle."

The prince seated himself on a large wingback chair to the left of the sofa, only a few feet from the ladies. Wentworth stood at attention off to the side, as if awaiting the prince's further instructions. Prince Reginald asked if they'd like more tea or cookies.

"Oh no, thank you. The tea and cookies were wonderful." Tina spoke as Lucy nodded in agreement.

Wentworth exited the room and Tina was curious what would happen next, but to her relief there were no awkward moments of silence. The prince explained that he would've asked his father to join them had he not been ill.

"We're sorry to hear that he's been sick. We will pray that he gets well soon." Tina hoped her words sounded sincere, because she genuinely hoped the elderly man would recover completely.

A bit of sadness clouded the prince's eyes.

"Thank you. I will admit I do worry about him as he gets older, but I'm thankful he does as well as he does. He still keeps up with all his royal obligations, even when he's advised to rest more." His face brightened as he gestured to some other paintings on the parlor walls. "Would you ladies be interested in seeing a few more paintings?"

"Oh yes, please," both women chorused as they stood.

Just then, a plump black and white cat sauntered into the parlor, giving the women a curious stare before rubbing against the prince's leg. "Ah, there you are, Ludwig. I wondered how long before you'd be joining us." A jovial laugh came from the prince, as he leaned down and rubbed the feline's chin.

Both women exclaimed over the handsome feline, and Lucy asked if they could pet him.

"Of course. Ludwig would enjoy the extra attention. Not that he lacks attention being a castle cat. We have another cat who resides with us. Daisy is most likely napping at the moment. She's not quite as sociable as Ludwig." The prince shook his head as the women cooed over Ludwig and stroked the cat's smooth fur.

Tina decided not to mention that she'd met the feline on her previous visit inside the castle. No need for a reminder about her fainting episode.

The next twenty-five minutes seemed to fly by as the prince pointed out different paintings and gave a brief background of each. He also wove in a bit of Felinia's history as he spoke. It was fascinating to Tina, and she was thankful her earlier nervousness had lessened. She could tell that Lucy was also taking in every detail, obviously as fascinated as Tina.

"Would you like to see the castle library?" The prince's eyes held an amused glint.

"Oh, yes," both women exclaimed at the same time.

Tina had always loved libraries, but she had never seen one in a castle turret. It was spectacular, with countless books filling every shelf of the rounded turret walls. Nestled in the center stood two velvet chairs and two small tables with petite lamps and a vase of fresh flowers. Tina practically swooned, mesmerized by the library.

All too soon, Wentworth joined them again in the hallway, informing the prince that the shuttle had arrived to return the guests to their hotel. Prince Reginald thanked his assistant before turning to the ladies with an almost-apologetic expression on his handsome face.

"I'm so sorry our visit must end now. Wentworth keeps me on schedule, which I'm sure is a good thing. But sometimes I wish I didn't have so many meetings to attend." He chuckled and shrugged, making Tina more aware of his well-built physique. Apparently, the prince must get adequate exercise to maintain his build.

As they bid the prince goodbye at the castle's side door, Tina again felt the strong yearning she'd had the previous time she'd been there. She longed to stay with Reginald at the castle, but that was ridiculous. She didn't belong there and was certainly not royalty. In fact, she was quite certain there was not a trace of royal blood in her lineage at all.

Tina started to follow Wentworth along the cobblestone path to the wooden gate, but the prince reached out and gently grasped Tina's arm. Startled, she swung around to face him and peer up into his dark eyes.

Prince Reginald leaned in a bit closer and spoke softly, "Thank you for being my guests today. I enjoyed seeing you again and meeting your friend. Would it be possible to remain in contact with you, Tina?"

She might as well collapse right there, because her insides had melted. Had she heard him correctly? Tina couldn't suppress the wide grin that formed. With a nod, she whispered, "Oh yes, that would be nice." She gazed up at him one more time, then turned and scurried along the cobblestones, doing her best not to trip and fall in her rush to join Lucy on the shuttle.

The women were again the only passengers. They gazed out the window for a parting glimpse of the beautiful stone castle and surrounding grounds. Wentworth had already returned to the side entrance, and the prince had remained inside the castle walls.

But as the shuttle pulled away, Tina couldn't help feeling that maybe—just maybe—she had found her handsome prince. And he truly *was* a prince.

~ ~ ~

Chapter 8

Wentworth was obviously troubled as Reginald shared about his visit with Tina and her friend the day after they'd visited the castle. But being the trusted assistant, Wentworth needed to know even private details of the prince's life. However, Reginald often wished the man would show a bit more emotion rather than taking everything so seriously.

But as his father had often reminded him, the fact that Wentworth was so proper and regimented made him an extremely devoted assistant, which was what they needed. Still, it would've been easier on Reginald when he opened up to Wentworth about Tina if the older man were a bit more relaxed.

"Sire, with all due respect, have you considered this matter thoroughly?" As soon as the words left the assistant's mouth, he blushed and ducked his head, as if afraid he'd spoken out of place. He hastily added, "I mean no disrespect at all, Your Highness. I realize this is your personal life."

Reginald almost laughed at the remorseful

expression on his assistant's face. "No disrespect taken, and I know you have my best interests at heart. But I hope to remain in contact with Miss Ransom, and perhaps get to know her better. Which, given the fact there are oceans and countries separating us, it might be quite the challenge."

"Yes, Sire. And I will do whatever I may to assist you in your endeavors. I only want to make certain you remain cautious in your pursuit of knowing the young lady better. And of course, discuss it with your father, the king."

Assuring Wentworth that he would certainly be discussing the matter with his father, Reginald was relieved when the assistant exited his office. Now he sat at his desk, gathering his thoughts and praying. Was he making a mistake being seriously interested in a lady from America? Not to mention the fact they'd only been in each other's company a total of three times, and that included the time Tina was recovering from a fainting spell. Not exactly prime visiting time.

Yet, he couldn't help but think of the signs that a relationship with Tina was possibly meant to be. The emergency landing her flight made on Felinia, then the fact she became ill and fainted in front of the castle, and also that she was able to return a few months later and visit Felinia again.

To his great relief and answered prayers, Reginald noticed that his father was improving and recovering from his pneumonia. Although he still had a lingering cough, it wasn't nearly as deep and rattling as it had been. The medicine and bedrest had helped a great deal.

Since the king was improving, Reginald felt it would be okay to talk with his father about Tina.

Specifically, his feelings for Tina and his hopes for a possible relationship. He uttered a hasty prayer before beginning his spiel.

The king listened with a curious expression on his tired face, but his eyes soon brightened. "Well, my son. This is all quite interesting." He slowly stroked the whiskers on his chin.

Waiting to see if the king commented further, Reginald sat with clasped hands and leaned forward in his chair. His father spoke in a serious tone. "I am assuming you've prayed about this young lady and a possible relationship with her?"

"Oh yes, Father. I've prayed a lot about this. Especially after what I've been through with Miss DeVenes. I would not want to repeat that mistake. Ever."

The king eyed him and nodded. "Given the fact you live in a castle, there are not abundant opportunities for you to meet young ladies. Especially appropriate ladies, Christian, well-groomed, and willing to abide by certain standards. You've only been in the company of Miss Ransom a few times, isn't that correct?"

"Yes, Sir." Reginald nodded, hoping this conversation wasn't taking an unintended turn.

"Also, given the fact Miss Ransom lives in America, if there is even a slight possibility that she may be the one God has for you, then you'd need to be in her company more than a few times. My suggestion is to invite her to visit Felinia again as a guest of the castle. The two of you could become better acquainted as you have chaperoned visits." The king's cough unfortunately began again, indicating his father had reached his limit for that day.

"Thank you, Father. I respect and agree with your suggestion, and I will make plans to invite her soon. I'm going to summon Genevieve for your cough medicine and perhaps some soothing tea with honey. You need to rest." Reginald gazed at his tired father. He only hoped he hadn't talked with his father too long, because he still needed much rest to recover from his illness.

After seeing that his father was settled, Reginald returned to his office to send an email to his closest friend. Xavier Johnson and Reginald had met in college, and they'd become pals right away. Although Xavier was married now and lived in London, the men had remained in contact and even managed to visit every few years. Reginald longed to update his buddy on the American he'd met, but it might be best to wait. He didn't want to sound like a schoolboy, pining after a crush.

Later that day, Reginald received a phone call from Xavier. He couldn't resist grinning as he heard his friend's exuberance. "I decided to phone instead of emailing, Reggie. Your note piqued my curiosity, and I have a feeling there's something you're not sharing with me."

"Why would you think that?"

"Because we were roommates in school, and are still close friends, although miles apart. Your note sounded rather stiff, as though you were trying to keep something from me. I just hope nothing is wrong." Genuine concern in Xavier's admonition prompted Reginald to open up.

Choosing his words carefully, Reginald briefly recounted his first meeting with Tina in the airport, her fainting spell at the castle, and his visit with Tina and her friend for tea. He also mentioned the cloud hanging over him with the false accusations about his broken betrothal to Lorie.

Xavier encouraged him to pursue a friendship with Tina and to ignore the negative publicity in the tabloids. "Anyone who knows you will certainly know those statements are false, Reggie. Outright lies."

After talking about twenty more minutes, their call ended, with Xavier promising to visit Felinia within the year. Reginald was amazed at how the call had lifted his spirits. He thought about Tina and her best friend Lucy. They seemed like genuinely close friends. Perhaps a prince needed a close friend, too, so he was thankful for Xavier. If anything did develop with Tina, he'd be sure to update his buddy in London right away.

~ ~ ~

On their last full day on the island, Tina and Lucy headed out to explore and shop. Both women were still feeling a bit dazed after their wonderful visit at the castle the previous day, but they agreed to forestall discussing their amazing experience until their flight home. For now, they needed to take advantage of seeing all they could in this tropical paradise.

"I hope we don't get caught in a storm today. We've been so fortunate having good weather so far." Lucy cast an anxious glance up at the sky, where puffy clouds were gathering.

"You're right. I thought it was interesting when Prince Reginald told us how blessed the island has been over the years in escaping hurricanes. But he also said that now and then they do have a strong thunderstorm with blustery winds." Tina was glad she'd brought along a small umbrella, just in case.

The women visited various island shops, delighted with their purchases of jewelry and a few gifts. They returned to their favorite café for lunch before continuing their exploring. As they walked along and chatted, they soon realized they'd gone farther than they'd planned.

"Um, this area doesn't look like where we've been. Look, there's the port up ahead. Should we go that far, or turn around?" Lucy's worried tone let Tina know her friend was nervous. Maybe they should turn around.

"Yes, you're right. Let's just get a little bit closer to the port so I can snap a picture, okay? We haven't seen this part of the island at all." Tina was glad when her friend agreed.

Moving closer to the port gave them an entirely different view of the island. Not a paradise at all, but a small area with run-down, small houses, some resembling shacks. The friends were silent as they viewed their current surroundings. This must be the area that the woman on the shuttle had cautioned Tina about on her previous visit, and it made her feel sad.

After snapping a photo of some boats docked at the port, Tina startled as she heard a low rumble of thunder.

Lucy's eyes widened. "Uh oh. When you can hear thunder, lightning follows. We'd better head back."

"Yep, I'm right with you." Tina put her camera away and made sure her umbrella was ready to pull from her bag, if needed. The wind picked up as the women turned around and headed back, walking at a clipped pace rather than their previous relaxed stroll.

A man who appeared in need of a shower sat with a bowl in front of him, obviously a beggar as he called out to passers-by. Only one person tossed coins into his bowl. From everything Tina could see, he didn't appear to be handicapped, at least not physically handicapped. Every few seconds he'd shout out.

Abruptly, Tina stopped, reached into her bag and then looked at her friend. "I'll be right back." She trotted to the beggar, placed some coins into the bowl, and offered a quick greeting. "God bless you, sir. Have a good evening." The sun would be setting before too long, so hopefully the beggar wouldn't sit there after dark.

Lucy watched her with a sympathetic smile. "You have such a good heart, girlfriend. Who knows what that man will spend the money on." She shook her head and squeezed her friend's arm.

With a shrug, Tina replied. "I know, but for some reason I just couldn't keep walking without doing something." She lifted up a quick prayer for the beggar, then walked in silence beside her friend until they were back in the familiar section of the island.

"Ugh, I hate to even say this, but after being in that other area, I need a nice, warm shower." Lucy shook her head.

"Yeah, I know what you mean." Tina agreed, yet she couldn't help wondering about that section of the island. Did the king or prince ever visit those people? No matter how dazzling a place might be, there were still bound to be areas of poverty and crime. She had a feeling that Felinia was no different, even though it still seemed a bit magical to her. And sadly, it was almost time to leave this magical place and return home.

Even if she was never able to return, she'd forever treasure the memories of this beautiful island and meeting the prince. But she'd pray to return some day, because this tiny island had captured a piece of her heart. And although she didn't want to admit it, the prince had captured a piece of her heart, too.

~ ~ ~

A note from Tina arriving in that day's mail was exactly what Reginald needed. The scandal that had broken out after Lorie DeVenes issued lies about him was a huge blow, not to mention the effect it could have had on his father if the staff hadn't protected the older man from the news.

Thankfully, Wentworth informed the staff that while King Franklin was recovering from his illness, they were to refrain from spreading the ridiculous, fabricated story about the prince and Lorie DeVenes. Reginald was yet again thankful for the assistant's loyalty and devotion to the royal family.

Seated in his favorite chair next to the large window overlooking the courtyard, Reginald took in the serene view of colorful flowers and the bird feeders gently swaying in the breeze. So peaceful, much as his life used to be.

How things had changed. Now he longed to be free of scandalous reports, especially since they were complete lies. *Vengeance is mine, saith the Lord.* Part of a Bible verse popped into his mind, reminding him that the Lord was in control over this entire situation. Justice would eventually prevail over the lies and innuendos.

But in the meantime, Reginald must deal with the feelings of indignation and anger that waged a battle within him. To think that he'd actually been betrothed to the woman behind this scandal almost made him queasy.

Reginald switched his gaze from the scene in the courtyard to the note in his lap. He was eager to read what Tina had written, and wished she was seated beside him at this window right now. Maybe one day...but he'd try to refrain from getting his hopes up.

As he read the words written in Tina's feminine penmanship, he could almost hear the gentle drawl in her soft voice. He read her expressions of gratitude, thanking him for the hospitality shown to her and Lucy. Reginald smiled at her comments about the beauty and charm of the castle and the gardens. It was obvious she had a genuine appreciation for the history and elegance of the castle—almost a fascination, it seemed.

After reading the note once, Reginald re-read it until he almost memorized it. Without giving the action any thought, he brought the pastel pink note card to his mouth and kissed it. What was he doing, kissing a piece of paper? At least Wentworth wasn't nearby—his assistant would surely think he'd gone mad.

An unwelcome thought forced its way to the front of his mind. Would the scandal that had come forth, thanks to Lorie DeVenes, cause a problem if and when Tina visited Felinia again? Especially if she visited in the near future, which is what Reginald hoped and prayed for. Perhaps if she stayed at the castle for this visit and out of the eye of the public, no one would be aware of her presence and the tabloids wouldn't drag her into the muck of their ridiculous lies.

The recognizable tapping from Wentworth at his office door snapped him from his musings. "Enter, please."

The assistant entered, bowed slightly, then looked directly into Reginald's eyes. "Your Highness, pardon the interruption if you were having a moment of quiet reflection, but Collins has informed me that Miss DeVenes has been confronted about the horrible stories that have been printed." He paused, allowing time for his words to sink in.

"She denies being the source of those stories, which we certainly know are all lies. Begging your pardon, Sire, but I am wondering if perhaps she feels guilty and is hoping the entire ugly matter will disappear." Disdain colored Wentworth's words as he shook his head.

"Thank you, Wentworth. How interesting that Miss DeVenes is denying the matter. And who knows? Maybe she's innocent and another person started the entire ridiculous story." Reginald's eyebrows arched as he shrugged. Somehow, he couldn't quite believe that Lorie DeVenes was an innocent victim of this crazy scandal.

"Begging your pardon, Sire, but I highly doubt the woman is innocent."

"You may be right. And you probably are. It just makes me sad to think that someone I had planned to marry has turned against me so." Reginald shook his head and stretched his tired shoulders.

"Well, Sire, she's likely not turned against you, but rather feels scorned. I've always heard that some women know no limits when they feel scorned." Wentworth's face had reddened as though embarrassed to have offered an opinion about a subject they didn't talk about.

Reginald couldn't resist a chuckle, knowing the assistant's comments were well-intended. "Thank you, Wentworth. You could be right." Eager to change the subject, he broached the topic of inviting Miss Ransom back to the castle, explaining the particulars that he and his father had discussed.

"Having her remain here as a guest of the castle would not only allow us to become better acquainted, with chaperoned visits, of course, but would also shield her from the horrible stories circulating."

Wentworth appeared to be listening, and to Reginald's pleasant surprise, the man nodded. "That all sounds like a good plan, Your Highness. I'm happy that you've discussed this with your father. I deeply value and respect his thoughts, so if he is agreeable, then I'm supportive of whatever the two of you wish to do. And I will support Miss Ransom's visit and do all I can to help, Sire." He inclined his head.

Suddenly things were looking brighter, despite the sickening tabloid stories about Reginald's unfaithfulness to Lorie DeVenes and the threats he'd made against her. He still prayed that the people of Felinia would continue to support the royal family and see the truth.

But at the moment, he had no time to dwell on a scorned woman's fabricated tales, because of a certain young lady in America. A lady who hopefully would be visiting the castle again very soon.

~ ~ ~

The week following the visit to Felinia, Tina had

trouble returning to her regular routine. Although she loved her job, her mind kept replaying memories of her trip—especially the visit with Prince Reginald at the castle.

Tina was especially thankful the trip had gone so well for Lucy's sake. After her bestie had missed their original trip to Italy, Tina had wanted to make sure this excursion was a fun adventure, and judging from Lucy's exuberance, it had been.

October had arrived, bringing cooler weather along with autumn leaves. Tina checked her mailbox one afternoon, her mind on upcoming activities she'd do with her kindergarten students. When she lifted out an envelope from Felinia, she almost dropped it, then ran back inside her apartment to read the note.

Her eyes brimmed with tears as she read the greeting. *My dear Tina.* How sweet. Did he really feel that way? Could it be possible that she really was dear to Prince Reginald, even though they still hardly knew each other? She continued reading the note, then read it again and again in disbelief. He was inviting her to visit Felinia again, but instead of staying at the hotel, he was inviting her to be a guest at the castle! Was she dreaming?

She had an urge to hop in her car and drive to Lucy's apartment, simply to ask her friend to read the note and make sure she wasn't imagining the message. But no, upon re-reading it for the sixth time, there was no mistaking it. The prince was inviting her to be a guest at the castle. What should she do?

Pray. Tina closed her eyes as she sat down on her living room sofa and poured her heart out to the Lord. Even though He already knew her innermost thoughts and longings, Tina still had a sense of peace as she told the Lord how she'd been feeling.

Minutes later, she phoned Lucy, who'd recently adopted two precious kittens and was eager to tell about their latest antics. After listening, Tina attempted a casual tone as she shared details of her note from the prince.

"Girlfriend, this is super exciting! Why didn't you tell me this as soon as you phoned?"

"I wanted to hear about Puff and Pocahontas," Tina giggled. "They're so adorable, and since I love cats too, I wanted to hear about them. Besides, since I can't have a cat in my apartment, I plan to enjoy your kitties."

"So, when does the prince want you to visit again? Don't leave any details out—tell me everything." Lucy's excited tone made Tina smile. She couldn't imagine having a better friend.

"The prince mentioned that he wouldn't want to take time away from my students, which was thoughtful. He also mentioned that with the holidays coming up, he didn't know if I'd want to visit so soon, but since I'd be out of school anyway...I don't know what to do." Tina's mind was whirling. So much to consider, not the least of which would be the financial aspect of another flight. At least she wouldn't have a hotel expense, though.

Was she crazy even to consider this? Kindergarten teachers from small towns in Tennessee didn't meet charming princes and live happily ever after. Did they? It all seemed unreal. A dream that might be setting her up for major heartbreak.

When Lucy's boyfriend arrived for supper, the

call ended. Tina went ahead and phoned her brother, trusting his wisdom and guidance. Initially, he sounded shocked, but the more she told him, the more he leaned toward advising her to return to Felinia. "Nothing to lose," he'd said the words half-jokingly and half-seriously. He even assured her that if she was gone during the holidays, it would be fine. "We'd miss you, but this is a great opportunity for you, sis."

That evening, Tina wrote a reply to Prince Reginald, thanking him for his invitation. She added that visiting during her December break might be an option, but she certainly didn't want to interfere with his Christmas plans. After second-guessing her wording, she finally was satisfied and sealed the envelope to mail the next day. Now she'd have to work hard to remain focused on her students and her routines as she awaited a reply.

She'd also need to refrain from reading tabloids that might post lies about the prince and his ended betrothal. That would accomplish nothing except to cause doubts to form in Tina's mind. No one was perfect, of course, but she just couldn't imagine Prince Reginald being capable of those accusations. Infidelity and threats—those *had* to be lies.

Pray. The reminder came again, so Tina searched Scriptures to calm her soul. She located one of her favorites in the Psalms. *I will instruct thee and teach thee in the way which thou shalt go.* She read and re-read the verse. Yes, she knew without a doubt that the Lord would show her clearly which way to go.

~ ~ ~

Would she be able to return to Felinia for a visit?

Prince Reginald hoped and prayed, and then suddenly a thought hit him between the eyes. Most likely Tina was not a wealthy woman, given the fact she was a kindergarten teacher. Surely the expense of flying overseas had to take a toll on her savings, although he had no idea whatsoever about her personal finances.

But if he ventured a guess, he'd say that she was not wealthy by any means. What if she wanted to return to his country for a visit but couldn't afford it? How should he handle this issue tactfully without causing embarrassment to her?

Discussing the matter with his father that afternoon, the king nodded thoughtfully. "Yes, son. That could be a tricky situation. But I see no other way to handle it than to pay for her flight expenses. She's coming as a guest of the castle, as if we were entertaining a foreign dignitary. Perhaps if you present it in that manner, Miss Ransom will be open to allowing you to pay for her flight. You certainly don't want to offend her." A rattling cough started in his chest, and the king sat back in his large leather chair.

Reginald didn't want to tire out his father discussing his possible love life. Reginald patted his father's shoulder and told him he'd summon tea and that he needed to rest.

After Genevieve brought tea and a snack of cheese and fruit for King Franklin, Reginald left his father's office and returned to his own. Waiting for mail to travel back and forth would be too time-consuming, so there was only one thing to do. Reginald would have to make a phone call to Tina, and he hoped it wouldn't be awkward.

Fortunately, Wentworth stopped by his office

shortly after making that decision to phone Tina, so Reginald asked him to help determine the time difference. He didn't want to phone her during the middle of the night. After checking online, the assistant informed the prince that the next hour should be an appropriate time to place the call.

Thankfully, Wentworth didn't remain in Reginald's office, so the privacy and quiet surrounding him enabled him to think about his words as he jotted them on paper. He finally decided on a way to get his point across without sounding blunt. He also didn't want Tina to feel like a charity case.

Sending up another prayer that his words would be well-received, Reginald placed the call. As he listened to the ringtone, he wondered if he was getting worked up for nothing. For all he knew, Tina might not even be home. After all, she likely led a busy life.

On the fourth ring she answered, sounding a bit breathless. When she realized it was him, Reginald heard the surprise in her voice and could imagine a sweet smile on her face. At least he hoped she was smiling. She explained her breathless state was due to watering some plants by her front door and rushing inside the apartment to grab her phone.

He chuckled and assured her it was fine. "I guess I should've let you know I'd be calling, but by the time we wait for letters to travel back and forth across the ocean, it takes a while."

"I'm glad to hear from you, and I hope you and your father are doing well." Even from another country, Reginald could hear the sweetness in her tone.

"Yes, thank you. My father is improving from pneumonia, and I'm doing well. Except for the ridiculous so-called news reports in some of the papers." He forced an awkward laugh but wondered if he was making a mistake in mentioning the incidents. But surely she must know about Lorie DeVenes' false accusations.

"Um, yes…I did see a little bit on the internet. But I realize that not everything that's reported online is true." She spoke the words with no accusation in her tone.

Reginald was relieved at her response, but he felt he needed to clear the air before she flew to Felinia. He didn't want anything to mar her visit, nor stand in the way of their relationship growing, if it was the Lord's will.

Keeping his tone level, Reginald hoped he could say everything necessary and keep their call upbeat. "Yes, that's for certain. And in this case the accusations against me were completely untrue. All lies. It's a disturbing situation. As I'm sure you're aware, I was betrothed to Miss DeVenes. Thankfully, the Lord placed it on my heart to end the engagement."

He paused, hoping he hadn't completely scared Tina away. At her silence, he continued, "Anyway, I thought our families could remain on good terms even though Miss DeVenes and I were no longer betrothed. But apparently, she became bitter and spread fabricated stories about me. I will admit this has angered me and also hurt my heart. However, being a Christian man, I must forgive and not seek revenge."

Before he could say more, Tina spoke in a gentle tone. "I'm so sorry you're going through this, and I cannot imagine a woman doing such a spiteful thing, no matter how hurt she might feel. I will pray that all the false stories will stop, and people will know that you are innocent." Her words were like a soothing balm to his spirit, making him even happier that he'd phoned her.

"Thank you, Tina. Hearing you say that means a great deal to me. Now, on to a much happier topic." He paused and was glad to hear a small chuckle from her. "I want to let you know that since this will be another overseas trip for you, we will gladly pay for your flight. Consider yourself a special guest of Felinia Castle. To be honest, my father suggested this, and I wholeheartedly agreed with him." He continued with a few more details, and when he stopped talking, he heard a small gasp.

"I-I don't know what to say. I'm very honored and thank you for the offer. But I don't think it would be right for you to pay for my flight expenses."

"Oh, but I insist. Actually, my father does too. You wouldn't argue with a king, would you?" He laughed, relieved when she joined in.

"Well, if you phrase it that way, I guess it wouldn't be proper for me to argue with a king. Especially since you've been so kind to me."

They discussed the details for a few more minutes. When the call ended, Reginald realized he was beaming. And why shouldn't he? Tina Ransom was coming to visit him, and Lord willing, this would be the start of a real relationship with her.

~ ~ ~

Chapter 9

"Are you serious? This is all wonderful, Tina." Lucy was beside herself with excitement when Tina shared the news of her upcoming trip to Felinia. She knew she could trust her best friend, so she confided about her flight expenses being covered by the prince, and that she'd be staying in the castle as a guest.

"So, you'll basically have a free trip to a beautiful island country across the ocean. And at Christmastime." Lucy sighed dreamily and then reached over and hugged her friend. They had just left Tina's apartment for pizza, but at the moment Tina wasn't sure she could eat a bite due to her stomach doing happy somersaults.

"You're right. This will basically be a free trip. I just can't believe it." She hesitated. "Do you really think I'm doing the right thing in going?"

Lucy swung her around to look directly into her face. "I am positive you're doing the right thing. Think of this as a gift from God. What a wonderful opportunity for you to visit the royal family, and who knows what might develop. Just don't forget your peasant friends when you become a queen someday." Lucy giggled through the tears brimming in her eyes. "I am so happy for you, girlfriend."

Tina had a hard time suppressing the tears herself. "I'm glad you think I'm doing the right thing. And as for me forgetting my friends, you know I'd never do that. Especially not you—you're the best." As if suddenly realizing what else her friend had said, Tina giggled. "It just hit me that you said I might become the queen someday. Wow, you have big hopes for me, don't you?"

The two women talked and laughed as Tina drove them to the Blueberry Cove Pizza Eatery. Tina kept thinking about how blessed she was having Lucy for her best friend and how sweet she'd been sharing in the excitement of what was happening in Tina's life. But suddenly Tina felt a niggle of guilt, because she didn't want her friend to feel left out. She quickly changed the topic and asked about Lucy's kittens and how her house hunting was going.

"Well, the kittens are doing great. You need to come and visit Puff and Pocahontas before you leave for Felinia." Lucy paused and offered a mischievous grin before continuing. "As for the house hunting, Rob is going with me to look at some houses this Saturday." A pink blush covered Lucy's face and Tina squealed.

"That's great, Lucy! So, you two must be getting along really well." She'd hoped Lucy and her longtime boyfriend would become engaged, because they seemed perfect for each other.

"Yep, we are. He's already talking about us spending lots of time together over the Christmas holidays. When I mentioned that I'm looking at houses, he offered to go with me. Should be interesting." She giggled.

Hearing this news from her best friend confirmed, in a way, that Tina was supposed to make another trip to Felinia. The women were so close and knowing that Lucy would be busy with her house search and her relationship with Rob, gave Tina more peace about her upcoming trip.

Now, if only her trip would be safe and her relationship with Prince Reginald wouldn't be awkward, things would be fine. As excited as she was, Tina needed to continue praying about all of it.

When the day arrived, her brother drove her to the airport and hugged her goodbye. She'd been unsure when she would be flying back home, and shrugged when her brother teased her. "Well, if there's a royal wedding make sure your brother is invited."

"I don't think you need to go that far. But you'll hear from me, don't worry. And I'll let you know when my return flight arrives. I sure appreciate your taxi service." She gave him another quick hug, fighting the sudden tears that threatened to cascade down her face. She'd never been away from family close to the holidays.

"Hey, that's what big brothers are for. You just stay safe and enjoy your time in a castle." He gave her another hug and a wink before she headed to her boarding area.

Thankfully, the flight to Atlanta and the connecting flight to Felinia were uneventful, and even though Tina attempted to rest a bit, she was too keyed up. She tried to imagine what it would be like staying in the castle, but she didn't have a clue. This time, hopefully, she'd be able to meet the king in person, but for the time being, she'd pray his health was improving.

About nine hours later, the plane began its descent to Felinia, and Tina's stomach also descended. She hoped she'd eaten enough so she didn't become sick. *Pray.* The whispered reminder let her know that she must pray for guidance and strength, and she'd be fine. Looking out her airplane window at the lush greenery of the island filled her with even more excitement. She drew in deep breaths to calm herself.

After landing and collecting her luggage in the small airport, Tina headed to the passenger pick-up area to look for Wentworth. What if she'd forgotten what he looked like? Her heart raced as she pulled her bag behind her, but suddenly a strong hand reached out and grabbed her luggage.

~ ~ ~

"My apologies, Miss Ransom. I didn't mean to startle you, but I was afraid you'd get away from me. I'm here to drive you to the castle." The tiniest sliver of a smile appeared on Wentworth's mouth as he bowed his head.

Tina thanked him and followed along as he pulled her baggage to the exit. Another man waited for them and ushered Tina into the waiting limousine. Wentworth placed her luggage in the back, then took his place inside the large vehicle. The ride to the castle went smoothly, Wentworth pointing out various places of interest they passed, including a small church built of stones. With stained glass windows, it reminded Tina of a scene from a painting.

Upon her arrival at the castle, she noticed a

section she'd not viewed before. The limo pulled up to a large door that Tina assumed was near the castle's kitchen, because when another guard opened the door, delectable aromas wafted out to greet her.

No sooner had she stepped into the carpeted hallway of the back entrance than Reginald appeared, and a smile spread across his face. He took both her hands in his, then asked about her flight and if she was tired. His dark eyes bore into hers, and she thought she surely must be dreaming.

Two maids hovered nearby, ready to assist her. Could this really be happening? She drew in another breath of the wonderful aromas from the kitchen. Yes, it was all very real, and she really was with a handsome prince in a castle.

"After you get settled, we will dine, and then I'll go over a few activities I thought we might do during your visit, if you'd like. Please know you won't offend me if I suggest anything that isn't to your liking." His eyes twinkled, making Tina wonder what he'd planned. Surely nothing like scuba diving in the ocean, she hoped.

She needn't have worried, though, because the activities were very much to Tina's liking. The couple enjoyed a scrumptious meal in the dining room, just the two of them. Reginald explained that his father was eager to meet her, but he wasn't dining with them due to having a slight cold. He assured her that it was nothing serious, but they were being cautious since he'd had pneumonia earlier.

After the meal, Reginald announced while there was still daylight, they'd take a drive around the small island so Tina could view more sights. Collins, the public relations man, drove the couple in his private car with tinted windows, so there was no chance anyone would notice them.

When Collins drove them to one of the beaches that afforded a lovely view of the turquoise sea, Reginald reached over and squeezed Tina's hand, sending tingles rushing through her. He grinned as he told her she'd need to visit again in the summer and enjoy one of their beaches.

Was it her imagination, or had the prince's gaze traveled to her lips? She mustn't get carried away. They still barely knew each other. To her relief, Collins spoke at that moment, asking the prince where he should drive next. Before returning to the castle, the prince pointed to another beach area, along with a charming neighborhood with lovely cottages. It was all so picturesque.

"Thank you for the island tour. I enjoyed seeing parts of Felinia I'd not seen before." Tina gazed up into Reginald's eyes after they're returned inside the castle.

"You are welcome. I know that wasn't terribly exciting, but at least you were able to see more of our island." He leaned down and scooped up a fluffy cat in his arms. "May I present to you, Daisy, our other resident feline." He gently stroked the gray and white cat, and she rewarded him with loud purrs and a look of sheer adoration.

Tina understood that look. Prince Reginald was easy to adore, and that startling realization was cause for concern.

~ ~ ~

Why did time have to pass so quickly when a

person was enjoying themselves? Reginald couldn't believe that Tina had already returned to her home in Tennessee, after spending a wonderful four days as a guest of the castle. For him, the time with her had been ideal.

Although he would've loved for Tina to spend Christmas in Felinia, it wouldn't be fair to her, as she needed to be with her family. When she'd mentioned her older brother, Reginald sensed there was a close bond there, and he even felt a tiny bit of envy. Being an only child, he'd always hoped that one day he would have several children, Lord willing.

Tina loves children. The thought popped into his mind—something else to add to his mental list of reasons she appealed to him so much. Actually, there were many reasons the American appealed to him, which made the fact they lived oceans apart even harder.

When he'd shared more of Felinia's history with her, she appeared genuinely fascinated by it. They'd pored over scrapbooks filled with photos and drawings from Felinia's past monarchs, and she'd laughed at his attempts at humor when he told stories about his ancestors' antics. There was just something so different about this woman—she seemed so *real*, causing Reginald to acknowledge the truth that Lorie had been putting on a show. Apparently, she'd been consumed with the idea of marrying into royalty, and Reginald had been her way to achieve that goal.

Wentworth's tapping at his door jolted Reginald out of his musings, serving as a reminder he had work to do. Even though his country was a tiny island nation, serving as the prince entailed numerous duties and obligations. He couldn't imagine how royals in larger countries managed everything, yet he supposed they had numerous staff members helping them.

"Excuse the interruption, Sire, but I needed to go over a few items on the upcoming schedule with you. Not the least of which is the Felinia Christmas parade, which is next week. And Collins also requests to meet with you regarding an article he's submitting to a publication. The article will shed a positive light on Felinia, telling about some of our Christmas festivities."

"Yes, that sounds like an excellent idea. Especially after the recent negative press." Reginald's gut tightened just thinking about the awful lies that had been printed. He didn't miss his assistant's scowl at the mention of those articles.

As he went through the motions and attended to his various duties and Christmas activities, Reginald couldn't keep his thoughts from returning time and again to the beautiful American he wanted to see again. When he'd mentioned that he would like to keep in touch with Tina, her face had brightened. Shortly before she'd left for the airport, he asked if she'd like to visit Felinia again in the springtime, and her immediate, positive response thrilled him.

Could this woman be the one that God had for him? There were too many miles between them, which seemed to be the only obstacle. But everything else seemed to point to the fact that there was a mutual attraction between them, despite their completely different backgrounds.

Reginald would keep praying. Since his father had seemed to like Tina, that was another plus. Never mind the fact that she was from America and didn't have a drop of royal blood in her—those details seemed insignificant, as far as Reginald was concerned.

What *was* significant was the realization that Reginald had feelings for Tina he'd never come close to having for Lorie. And to him, that was the biggest stamp of approval on a relationship with the auburn-haired beauty from Tennessee.

~ ~ ~

This could *not* be happening. Not again. Reginald fisted his hands and shook his head. This was definitely not how his new year should be starting off. Especially after a lovely Christmas season that included phone visits with Tina. She had loved the beautiful flowers he'd sent her, thanks to Wentworth having placed the order. And they'd even talked about future visits, with a possibility of Reginald traveling to the United States at some point.

And now *this.* Wentworth stood beside Reginald's desk, looking remorseful for having to share bad news. "Yes, Sire. It's despicable, and I hated being the one to notify you. But when Collins alerted me to the fact of more lies making the news—this time along with photos—I knew I must update you."

Reginald's head throbbed, and it was no wonder. The entire situation was absurd. Pictures of Reginald— obviously photo-shopped—insinuated he'd been cavorting in Italy with women during his betrothal to Lorie DeVenes. The entire situation was ludicrous.

"Rest assured, Your Highness, Collins is doing all he can to investigate and handle this matter. We will not have your excellent reputation nor Felinia's tarnished in any way. There's no doubt that Miss

DeVenes is behind this. Perhaps even her father is assisting, given the fact he's completely withdrawn from his projects with King Franklin."

Reginald knew that ties had been severed with Mr. DeVenes, and the king and prince agreed that was for the best. Now, after seeing more attempts to cast a negative light on the prince, Reginald was actually relieved that his father had no dealings whatsoever with the man. Good riddance.

The photos appeared authentic, no thanks to modern technology. But the fact that they were not authentic stirred up more anger in Reginald. He had no idea who the women were, and his head throbbed even more as he stared at images of himself smiling at various women. Preposterous!

Wentworth reached out to move the images away from the prince. "I hated wasting ink printing these, but when Collins alerted me to these articles with photos, I knew I must let you know right ahead. I'm truly sorry, Your Highness." The assistant rarely called Reginald by his royal term, but in matters of such a serious nature, it seemed fitting.

Reginald managed to offer a semblance of a smile to the loyal man. "It's certainly not your fault. You're only the messenger, and I need to be aware of this. I'm sure we'll be issuing a statement soon. We must assure the public these are all false." Perhaps it was time to take legal action—libel, defamation of character—but Reginald just couldn't think about that at the moment.

A far greater concern formed in his thoughts, one that made him feel even worse. *What if Tina sees these photos and reads the articles? Will she believe this garbage?* His gut clenched, but he knew what he must do. He'd try to assure Tina that none of this was true. Again. But would she believe him?

~ ~ ~

Tina's picture-perfect visit to Felinia—although brief—had been wonderful and arriving home to Blueberry Cove in time to celebrate Christmas with family had completed her delightful school break. She'd also had time to get together with Lucy to share details of her visit to the small island. When a vase of gorgeous flowers arrived from Prince Reginald on Christmas Eve day, Tina thought she must be dreaming.

Lucy had teased her, saying that Tina appeared to be floating on a happy cloud. And why shouldn't she? Her routine life had become more than exciting, with possible adventure on the horizon. Since the prince had left no doubt in her mind that he wanted to stay in contact with her as often as possible, Tina became almost giddy as she thought about the handsome, kind man.

Surely this must be a positive indication of how her new year would be. Lots of bright days ahead. She didn't even mind celebrating New Year's Eve in her small apartment alone, because Reginald had called her that afternoon. When the call ended, Tina released a contented sigh, knowing that one call meant more than all the dates with her ex-boyfriend, who thankfully had not contacted her again.

School had begun again in early January, and Tina was eager to do a lot of special winter projects with her kindergarten students as their learning progressed. Even her co-workers noticed her joy and teased her about being so cheerful on dreary-weather days.

On Friday afternoon, Tina arrived home and fixed herself a cup of hot chocolate, then turned on her laptop computer. She'd catch up on emails and news, then contact Lucy about meeting at the diner for lunch the next day. But as she viewed various emails and updates, she froze. A caption caught her eye, and she felt sick. No. She must be reading this wrong. It couldn't be.

But sure enough, a small article appeared with pictures of Prince Reginald and various Italian women. As Tina viewed them, her vision blurred with tears. This couldn't be real! Yet, the photos clearly showed a smiling Prince Reginald standing beside elegant women. Two of the photos showed the prince and one woman, but the other photos showed several women on either side of him, all smiling seductively at the handsome royal.

The sip of hot chocolate Tina had swallowed felt as though it had turned into a rock in her stomach. Afraid that she might become physically sick, she stood and raced to her kitchen sink, where she splashed cold water in her face. She needed to phone Lucy.

Minutes later, Lucy arrived at Tina's apartment, a small plate covered in foil and a box of tissues in tow. "You'll get through this, girlfriend. There has to be an explanation. Maybe those photos were taken a long time ago, before the prince and what's-her-name were engaged." Lucy gently led Tina to the small kitchen table, then set the plate in front of her. "I just baked these chocolate chip cookies after getting home from work. Now I know why I felt a nudge to bake them this afternoon." She offered Tina a sympathetic smile and a slightly warm cookie.

Tina took a small bite, hoping it wouldn't get

stuck in her throat along with the lump that had formed. Thankfully, the delectable cookie with gooey chocolate chips practically melted on her tongue. She'd forgotten what scrumptious cookies Lucy baked.

"So yummy. Thank you, my bestie." Tina looked up at Lucy, who grinned at her.

"Nothing like sweets to lift the spirits." Lucy sat in the chair across from Tina but didn't say any more, as though giving her friend the opportunity to vent if she chose.

After a few beats of silence, Tina sighed. "I just can't believe this. I should've known it was all too good to be true. I mean—he's a prince, so no telling how many women would be vying for his attention. And he's so handsome…and so nice…" Her voice trailed off as tears began to flow anew.

Lucy slid the box of tissues closer to Tina and patted her friend's hand. "Yes, I'm sure he is considered a very eligible bachelor, and tons of women would love to date him. But still…with all you've told me, and just from my own impression when we had tea at the castle, I can't help but think this is a set-up. That what's-her-name is so bitter that she's doing all she can for revenge."

Tina considered her friend's words. "You might be right. But what about those photos? You looked at them, too, and they look so real." Tears threatened again, but Tina managed to keep them at bay, thanks to Lucy's box of tissues.

"Didn't you tell me that the prince talked to you about future visits to Felinia? And he said he'd like to visit here at some point, right?" Lucy's questions caused Tina to feel a tiny bit of hope, but then the photo images stared back at her, again causing her spirits to plummet.

"Yes, he did. But I just can't stop thinking about those pictures." Tina shook her head, feeling drained. She was normally tired by Friday afternoons anyway, after a busy week with her kindergarten charges. But this was an emotional tiredness, that no amount of sleep would help.

"Okay, you need to try as hard as you can to stop thinking about those photos and focus on something else. I know it won't be easy, but maybe if you stay busy it'll help. Rob and I have a date tomorrow night, but other than that, I'm free. So, if you want to go shopping, out to eat, or whatever, I'm here." Lucy stared at her, a concerned look in her eyes.

Overcome by her best friend's kindness, she couldn't keep the tears from flowing again. Lucy thrust a tissue at her.

"You're the best, Lucy. I don't know what I'd do without you." Tina sniffled as she dabbed at her eyes.

"Well, no worries, because you're stuck with me, girlfriend. Besties for life." Lucy paused and grinned. "Now, decide what you'd like to eat this weekend, and we'll make plans. I've been wanting to try that new coffee shop that opened on Main Street, so we can stop in there if you want."

Tina's heart warmed at Lucy's kindness. No doubt about it—her friend was the best. Now, if she could only block those images, she'd do okay. But that was going to be a challenge. Because her spirits had gone from the highest to the lowest in a matter of an hour, and there was no denying how much it hurt.

~ ~ ~

Thanks to Lucy, Tina experienced some enjoyable moments as the two friends ate in the local diner, tried a newly-opened coffee place, and shopped in the Blueberry Cove gift shop. A few times, Tina even laughed as her bestie shared humorous comments several of her students had made.

But when Tina saw she'd missed a call from the prince, her good mood evaporated. A few hours later, he called again. Was he calling to ask if she'd seen the photos? Would he admit they were real, or maybe ignore the issue altogether? Tina didn't think she could keep a level tone while talking with him, and there was no way she'd allow herself to dissolve into tears while on the phone with him. Best to ignore his calls.

How had she gotten into this situation? Her life had been calm and orderly, and other than the break-up with Chuck a while back, she kept her life on an even keel. No extreme high or low moods. She'd assumed that eventually she'd meet someone and fall in love, but for the foreseeable future Tina had been content with her small-town Tennessee life. Then a chance meeting with a royal prince had changed all of that.

The following Monday morning, Tina immersed herself in her job. Another perk of teaching kindergarten was that her young students kept her so busy, it wasn't possible to think about much else.

During their lunch break, Lucy checked on her to see how she was faring. "You look like you're having a good day, girlfriend."

Tina nodded. "Yeah, I am. My little ones keep me busy—especially since one lost a tooth this morning.

Major kindergarten excitement." She grinned.

Later that afternoon, Tina opened her laptop for a few minutes after arriving home. She absolutely refused to look at any so-called news articles or photos concerning a tiny island to the west of Italy. But to her surprise, she had an email from Prince Reginald. Apparently, he'd given up on phone calls.

With trembling fingers, she clicked the email open, unsure of what to expect. Right away, Tina saw it wasn't brief, but not too terribly long, either. Her eyes swept over it as she tried to prepare herself for whatever it said.

The note opened with the usual pleasantries about how her new year was going and how much he'd enjoyed her brief visit before Christmas. Then he referenced the photos Tina had seen, and he wrote that he'd been angered and sickened over them. He emphasized that the photos were not real, but had been photo-shopped to appear as if he'd been with those women.

The prince went on to write that he'd assumed Tina had seen the false images, so he wanted to apologize, even though they weren't real. He added that his staff was working to uncover the source. It occurred to Tina that he didn't mention his ex-fiancée or her family. He ended his message by pleading with her to overlook any more photos or articles that might indicate he was involved with other women, and he assured her they were all lies. He'd even added that he would love to hear from her very soon.

After reading through the message, Tina re-read it, allowing his words to sink in. According to the prince, the photos were all fabricated. Did that mean he had enemies wanting to harm his reputation?

Rather than reply right away, Tina decided she'd discuss this note with Lucy first. It would be rude to ignore his email.

Tina's head felt as though it was spinning. This was too much. How had a kindergarten teacher from a small Tennessee town become involved with a prince across the world? A prince who was dealing with someone obviously trying to ruin his reputation. Maybe she shouldn't answer at all. But Tina knew she would, even though she wasn't sure what she'd say.

What remained a mystery to Tina was why a handsome prince on a beautiful, tropical island would be interested in an American teacher. They were not only from opposite sides of the world, but also opposite backgrounds. Tina had even joked with the prince that there was no royal blood in her lineage anywhere. Honest, hard-working citizens, but no royalty.

But what wasn't a mystery to her was how attracted she was to Reginald. Not only was he a handsome prince, but he also was genuinely kind. The few times she'd been in his presence, he had never made Tina feel like a commoner, nor did she feel uncomfortable being with him. There was no mistaking the chemistry between them, despite their totally different lifestyles.

Pray. The silent reminder sent a ripple of guilt through Tina. She'd not been doing enough praying about this situation. If she was meant to see Reginald again, and possibly have a real relationship with him, she needed to pray for guidance. And if she'd been mistaken about him, and those photos were real, then she needed to pray for discernment. She didn't think she could handle being deceived again, not even by a prince.

~ ~ ~

Reginald's emotions were on a roller-coaster ride. While relieved that his father's health had improved, he was still angry about the photos and the articles. All blatant lies.

Collins had been working hard to find the source and had been in touch with connections of the DeVenes family. But so far, he hadn't unearthed anything that involved the DeVenes, but he was determined to get to the bottom of the scandal. He'd also issued a press release from Felinia regarding the false photos and articles.

On top of everything else, Reginald had been more than a little disheartened when Tina refused to answer his phone calls, so in desperation he'd resorted to an email. Now all he could do was wait and hope she would respond.

When he'd viewed the photos of him and the women, his stomach clenched. While other men would likely consider the women attractive, they held no appeal for Reginald. There was only one woman who'd captured—and kept—his attention. And now he desperately wanted to see her again, as challenging as that might be to arrange.

Wentworth tapped at his door, reminding him of a meeting with his father in ten minutes. Since dignitaries were visiting Felinia within the coming months, Reginald must focus on his job as the prince of their small island nation. That should be his primary focus, if only his heart would remember that.

"Sire, do you have your notes for the meeting with the king? He wishes to see your ideas about the projected improvements for the west side of the island."

"Yes, I'll gather my notes and head to his office, Wentworth. Thank you." Reginald was thankful for his assistant's organizational skills, especially given how scattered his own thoughts were. He had no doubt that his preoccupied mind was obvious to Wentworth—and likely everyone else in the castle.

A nudge against his leg made Reginald look down and see Ludwig gazing up at him. The spoiled but affectionate cat wanted some attention, so Reginald stroked the feline's fur, the rumbling purrs a soothing balm to his nerves.

The meeting with his father went smoothly, although Reginald had to make himself focus on the items being discussed. As they were winding up, a sudden tapping at the king's door startled all three men.

When Wentworth answered, Collins rushed in, apologizing for the unplanned interruption. After the PR man shared his recent findings, it was no surprise he'd barged in on their meeting.

"My contacts on Italy's west coast have located the likely source behind the photos, and it seems that Mr. DeVenes is behind the scheme." Collins paused to catch his breath. He shook his head and continued, "I wanted to be thorough, because we don't need speculation. We need facts. And everything points to DeVenes." His eyes focused on the king, then on Reginald.

Once again, Reginald's gut clenched as it had when he'd first seen the absurd images. Breaking the silence that hung in the room, Reginald blurted out his first thought, "But why? Is this pure retaliation for breaking up with his daughter, or is there another motive?"

Collins nodded. "I'm afraid it appears to be both, Your Highness. Apparently, DeVenes is expecting payment for stopping the photos. In addition, Lorie DeVenes is still peeved that you ruined her plans to become a princess, and eventually a queen." He shook his head and scowled.

"It seems, according to my reliable informant, that Mr. DeVenes has been involved in some questionable financial dealings in Italy and needed to generate more income. After his daughter's heart was broken," Collins shrugged, "he saw an opportunity to exact revenge for her and make money for himself. Shameful."

Reginald let this information sink in. From everything their PR man had uncovered, it was obvious the DeVenes family was not an upstanding family after all. Quite the opposite. What a blessing he'd ended the engagement, or no telling what might've happened. A shudder ran down his spine.

As much discussion followed among the small group of men assembled in the king's office, Collins assured the king and prince they had enough evidence to start legal action. Apparently, DeVenes had made attempts to gain money in other unscrupulous ways.

Later, as Reginald headed to his own office to have tea in solitude and digest all the recent information, a stark and sobering thought popped into his head. If a marriage with Lorie DeVenes had taken place, Reginald would've married into a devious family. His father-in-law would've been a criminal. The very thought made him feel weak.

What a blessing he'd come to his senses and not gone ahead with a marriage. This was now total confirmation he'd done the absolute right thing in ending the betrothal, and he needed to lift prayers of thanks immediately.

~ ~ ~

The following week passed by with a flurry of activity for Reginald, including meetings, hosting some European guests in the castle, and receiving updates from Collins regarding legal matters concerning the false photos and articles. Yet, above all the activity, Reginald's thoughts—and heart—kept returning to one person. He'd still not received a reply from Tina, so he wasn't sure if she believed his explanation of the photos.

The following Saturday an email arrived in his inbox from Tina, and Reginald was beside himself. What if she wanted nothing more to do with him, and asked him to stop trying to contact her? He needed to face facts, so he opened the email and read, his pulse racing.

Her note was polite, but guarded. She admitted seeing the photos and articles, and how surprised she'd been. But she didn't acknowledge that she believed that they were all fabricated. She mentioned that she hoped his father was well, and that she'd been busy with her kindergarten students. Then she closed her note casually, wishing him well. That was it.

The email was not exactly cause for relief, but at least she'd not requested that he not contact her in the future. What could he do now? If only there weren't so many miles separating them. But that was the problem.

He couldn't very well show up at her doorway and plead with her to listen to him.

Daisy had padded into his office, and leaped onto his desk, situating herself beside his laptop. She gazed directly at him with her large, yellow eyes. Her purrs increased in volume as she continued staring at Reginald. Why did he get the feeling the cat was trying to tell him something?

He reached over with his right hand to rub the cat's soft fur, speaking gently to her as she purred. Then he re-focused on Tina's note, trying to think of how he could convince her of his innocence in the tabloid situation and that he cared about her. This entire situation must seem totally foreign to the kind of world she lived in. After all, she was a kindergarten teacher in a small town who spent her workdays with young children.

With Daisy's purrs continuing, Reginald thought about how much Tina loved cats, and how she'd lavished attention on Daisy and Ludwig when she was a guest in the castle. He also thought about how her green eyes lit up as she'd talked about the children in her class, and the activities she enjoyed with her students.

Yes, a different world, indeed. Seeing images of Reginald with various women, some gazing seductively at him in those photo-shopped pictures, must've been a jolt for her. And he could understand how she'd want no part of that kind of world.

He again turned his focus to the cat, still gazing at him. And suddenly, Reginald knew what he had to do. Regardless of how silly it might seem, he had to try. Because if there was any way he could convince the pretty American teacher to give him a chance, this just might do it.

~ ~ ~

The late January day's dreariness matched Tina's mood. She'd had a headache all morning, then one of her students became sick during lunch, and then the principal called a last-minute faculty meeting where he reminded the staff of inclement weather procedures.

Maybe it would snow, and everyone could have a day off, she hoped as her head throbbed. She loved being with her students, but with the way she felt today, a snow day was appealing.

When she arrived home, Tina brewed a small pot of coffee, hoping the caffeine would ease her headache. Then she opened up her laptop, ready to view something cheerful to lift her mood. Since she enjoyed plants, Tina went to a website that featured various houseplants and how to care for them. She was eager to add to her African violet collection and possibly one day even have a small backyard greenhouse—when she no longer lived in an apartment, of course.

Before shutting down her computer an hour later, Tina saw that an email had arrived from Prince Reginald. Her pulse quickened and she froze. Should she even read it? Steeling herself, she opened the email, unsure what she'd find. But she never would've expected what she saw.

The email featured photos of the castle cats, Ludwig and Daisy. There was a caption for each cat, as though they were speaking to Tina. *Please believe our Purr-ince* was underneath the photo of Ludwig, and below Daisy's photo was *Purr-ince Reginald is so sad and he misses you.*

Tina's hand went to her chest. The pictures were so cute and clever. She would've never imagined that Prince Reginald would send something like this, but she loved it. He must've known this would appeal to her love of cats. Surely, he would not have gone to such lengths if he wasn't sincere—and innocent. Would he?

Before Tina could decide how to respond, her cell phone rang, indicating a call from Reginald. Not hesitating, she answered right away, wanting to thank him for the pictures. Hearing his voice sent her heart racing, and a tingle rushed through her.

"Ludwig and Daisy would like to know if you received their email?"

Tina couldn't suppress a giggle. "Yes, I did. Please tell them I appreciate seeing their photos. Both cats are gorgeous."

"And what about their messages? They *purred* their hearts into those, and their words are true." His voice held a pleading tone, as though he was silently begging her to believe him.

As though a light was suddenly turned on in a dark room, Tina knew the truth. Those articles and the photos were all lies. Prince Reginald was innocent, and someone had made attempts to tarnish his squeaky-clean royal reputation. He'd tried to convince Tina by sending an email completely uncharacteristic of a prince. Yet, he'd known in her kindergarten teacher world, that would appeal to her—and it had.

"I believe them." Her simple admission caused a sigh of relief from the prince, and he chuckled.

"I am so thankful to hear that, Tina. This ordeal has been like a plague, and we're ready for the truth to be exposed. Which it should be, very soon, I'm happy to say. Thanks to diligent work by our public relations man and his contacts, everyone should soon realize those photos and articles were, in fact, all fabricated. Then all will be well in our little kingdom once again."

Tina could hear the sincerity in his voice, and that made her smile. But his next words made her heart soar.

"Now, let's talk about the next time you visit Felinia, which hopefully will be in the near future. And no worries, you'll again be a guest of the castle, so there will be no expenses on your part. All that's asked of you is to pay extra attention to two spoiled—but lovable—castle cats." A playfulness in Reginald's tone sent her pulse racing.

"Is that all?" Tina knew she must be grinning foolishly.

"Well, perhaps pay extra attention to a certain prince, too. If you don't mind, of course."

"I think that can be arranged. It sounds like a *purr*-fect visit to Felinia." Tina couldn't resist the play on words. Her heart was light, and she couldn't wait to return to the beautiful little island that had lots of felines, *and* the handsome Prince of Felinia.

Epilogue

Tina visited Felinia again on her spring break, and this visit was the best one of all, so far. Although guards and Collins remained close by, the couple took a leisurely stroll on a secluded beach on the east side of Felinia. When Reginald got down on one knee and proposed, Tina was overjoyed. Then he kissed her briefly but tenderly, and she was certain she would melt into the sand.

The couple decided on a royal wedding to take place in June. Tina was beyond thrilled at the unexpected turn her life had taken, and even though she'd now be living away from Blueberry Cove, Tennessee, that would always be home to her. She and Lucy promised each other that no amount of miles could dampen their friendship, and Tina knew they'd always stay in touch.

Thankfully, Tina was able to complete the school year, and looked forward to working with children in Felinia. She prayed that if the Lord was willing, one day she and Reginald would be blessed with a family of their own.

Reginald was in line to become the king of Felinia in the future, which meant that Tina would one day be the queen. Since Tina's maiden name was Ransom, he joked that his bride would be the king's ransom. She loved his sense of humor, and she looked forward to many years of laughter and making memories with this wonderful man, who now called her 'Princess' with affection.

Tina was in awe of how the Lord had orchestrated the events that led up to her becoming a member of a royal family. From the trip to Italy that had to make an emergency landing on a tiny island, to the present day as she planned a gorgeous royal wedding, Tina knew that only God could do such amazing work with details. She would spend the rest of her life serving the Lord and being the best royal wife she could be, and knowing that a small-town Tennessee girl really *could* become a princess.

The End

Author Patti Jo Moore is a lifelong Georgia girl who loves Jesus, her family, cats, and coffee. She's a retired kindergarten teacher who now writes "Sweet, Southern Stories" that always have a happy ending. When she's not writing or spending time with family (including her two precious grandgirls), Patti Jo can be found feeding cats—her six and any strays who visit her front porch. She loves connecting with readers and can be found on Facebook at Author Patti Jo Moore. You can also visit her at https://catmomscorner.blogspot.com   Patti Jo has 6 novels and 3 novellas, all published by Winged Publications (Forget-Me-Not Romance) and you can find her books on Amazon at Patti Jo Moore.

Follow her on Amazon here